HIS LIPS
BURNED ON HERS...

They tasted of wine and remorse and the sweetness of leashed desire. His arms around her were steely in their strength. Kelly felt the leap of the blood in her veins, felt her senses reel. As his kiss deepened, her soft lips parted She felt his hands smoothing over her back, drawing her closer, and she knew she was slipping into a sensuous lassitude where time and place and purpose ceased to exist . . .

More Romance from SIGNET

Captive
Kisses

Maxine Patrick

Ⓛ
A SIGNET BOOK
NEW AMERICAN LIBRARY
TIMES MIRROR

PUBLISHER'S NOTE

This novel is a work of fiction. Names, characters, places, and incidents are either the product of the author's imagination or are used fictitiously, and any resemblance to actual persons, living or dead, events, or locales is entirely coincidental.

COPYRIGHT © 1980 BY PATRICIA MAXWELL

SIGNET TRADEMARK REG. U.S. PAT. OFF. AND FOREIGN COUNTRIES
REGISTERED TRADEMARK—MARCA REGISTRADA
HECHO EN CHICAGO, U.S.A.

SIGNET, SIGNET CLASSICS, MENTOR, PLUME, MERIDIAN AND NAL BOOKS *are published by The New American Library, Inc., 1633 Broadway, New York, New York 10019*

FIRST PRINTING, SEPTEMBER, 1980

1 2 3 4 5 6 7 8 9

PRINTED IN THE UNITED STATES OF AMERICA

Captive

Kisses

❀ Chapter 1 ❀

There it was, the lake house. A rambling, white-painted structure with long expanses of veranda on three sides swathed in fine mesh screen, it sat beneath the shade of ancient live oaks hung with swaying gray strands of Spanish moss. Just beyond the house, half-hidden by the lush Louisiana undergrowth, was the guest cottage with its connecting walkway grown up with grass between the cracks. Both places were quiet, somnolent in the heat of the September afternoon. The only sound was bird calls from the leafy green canopy overhead and the distant hum of a motor far out on the tree-ringed lake.

Kelly Hartly sat in her small red car, looking at the house. She ran a hand through the gold-brown waves of her hair, a troubled frown between her clear gray eyes. The lake house was more isolated than she had remembered. Set on the back waters of Green Lake on a narrow peninsula of land at the end of a winding gravel road, its nearest neighbor was more than a mile away. Why hadn't she noticed before? The answer to that was this was the first time she had driven here by herself. All the other times she had been giggling and talking to Mary and Peter and Mark in the back of the

1

station wagon while Judge Kavanaugh drove. She hadn't cared how far it was, or how long it took to get there, as long as she was with the Kavanaugh family.

How long had it been since she was here? It must have been three years at least. The last time had been for the high school graduation party the judge and his wife had given for Mary's graduating class.

Mary Kavanaugh had been a good friend, still was, for that matter. It had been sweet of her to include Kelly in all those family outings, and kind of the judge and his wife to take up time with another awkward teen-ager, one who had no family. Kelly's father had been killed in an automobile accident when she was thirteen, her mother had died a few months later of cancer. Her teen-age years had been a trying time, living with an aunt who had a family of her own. The happiest moments she could remember had been spent at the lake house. Then on graduation she had earned a scholarship and moved away from the small town where the Kavanaughs lived. She had taken a two-year accounting course at college and found a job. After working for a year, she had earned a week's vacation, and she had thought to spend a part of it with Mary, catching up on everything that had happened since she had been gone. Being one of the last people hired at the firm where she worked, she had little choice in vacation dates. She had not minded taking her time off so late in the year, however, until she had discovered that the Kavanaughs had planned a trip to Europe for that period. They would leave a week before she reached town and return just as she was going back to work. When Kelly had spoken to her on the phone, Mary had been contrite, wailing in frustration. The European jaunt could not be postponed; it had been planned for months, and in addition scheduled for the two weeks just before court reconvened for the fall. At first, she had wanted to cancel her trip and stay, but Kelly wouldn't hear of it. Finally, after consulting with her mother, she had suggested that Kelly go down to the lake house. There Kelly could read to her heart's content, sun-bathe, swim, loaf, whatever. That was the only way Mary would be satisfied. She could not stand the thought of Kelly rattling around town with nothing to do. She wouldn't be able to enjoy herself unless she knew Kelly was having a good time, too.

It had sounded lovely, the sun-soaked days, the quiet. Kelly was not a boisterous type. She didn't particularly care for large crowds, noise, or loud music, and she loved to read, as Mary well knew. The peace, the long, endless summer days with Mary and her brothers, was what had appealed to her in the past. But now, as she sat in her car with perspiration popping out all over her from the sticky, ovenlike heat, it did not seem like such a good idea. There was something disturbing in the silence that lingered around the lake house, something that set her nerves to tingling and made her search the shadows beneath the trees with her eyes.

She was being silly. There was nothing there. The track of a drive that led down to the house had been overgrown with grass and weeds. No one had been near the place since the early spring, according to Mary. They didn't come down here, forty miles from their home, so much anymore, not since the boys, Peter and Mark, had left college and taken jobs out of the state and Mary had begun a promising career as a painter. They were all scattered, getting on with their lives. The judge still fished for crappie and bass now and then, but he had been told by his doctor to take it easy, not go out alone in a boat. Utilities for the year round and taxes, to say nothing of upkeep, were making it burdensome to hold on to a place they had little use for any longer. According to Mary, her mother and father had been thinking of selling.

There was no use sitting here, making herself jumpy and nostalgic by turns over something she couldn't

3

help. The sun would be setting soon, and she had to unpack the car, put away the groceries she had brought, turn on the air conditioning, and manage some sort of meal for herself. She would also like to have a quick, cooling swim if the raft anchored out from the shore was still floating. She couldn't see it from here because of the screen of cypress trees and willows that grew out into the water, though she could see the fishing pier. At least that long, wooden catwalk looked to be in good shape.

Kelly stepped from the car and closed the door. She stretched, stiff from sitting for the long drive, a slender figure in shorts and a top of salmon-colored cotton terry, worn with natural straw sandals. The first thing she had better do was let herself inside. That had been troubling her ever since she had spoken to Mary on the phone. She had said in passing that the extra key was in the usual place. As far as Kelly knew, that was under the fern tub that sat beside the steps of the side door, but after so long a passage of time it was possible the hiding place had been changed.

She knelt beside the tub with its trailing green fronds, lifting one corner. The heavy wooden half-barrel tilted obligingly on its brick supports. She felt underneath, running her hand as far as she could reach.

There was nothing there, no small metal box such as the judge had always produced. Picking up the end of a tree limb that lay nearby, Kelly raked further back under the tub. Still nothing. Getting to her feet, she stood with her hands on her hips. She should have known better than to take such an important detail for granted. If she had only thought to ask—but she hadn't.

With the fine curves of her mouth set in a firm line, Kelly opened the screen door of the side porch, and stepped inside. She felt over the side door, around the outside light fixture, and lifted the door mat. She even tried the door handle. With a defeated sigh, she moved back outside. All right. She didn't like to do it, but she had no choice. There was another way into the house.

Moving around to the back side of the house, facing away from the lake, she came to the windows that corresponded to the large bedroom where she and Mary had always slept. There had been a sash that didn't lock. Kelly and Mary had never worried about it, nor had the judge. Crime was practically nonexistent that far from civilization. There was no danger while so many people were in residence, and scarcely more when the house was empty. There had never been any problem with burglaries on the lake, not even with the house being as distant from its neighbors as it was. However, the judge maintained that a determined criminal would make short work of any lock or window glass, and that there was no use frustrating him unnecessarily. There was, in any case, nothing of any great value at the lake house to steal. It was furnished for comfort and durability, with the destructiveness of teen-agers in mind rather than style, beauty, or expense.

The window was too high for her to reach, even after she had found a screwdriver in the glove compartment of her car. It took a minute more to locate a cinder block, left over from the judge's barbeque grill project, to use as a stepping stool. It was only high enough if she turned it on end. Standing on that precarious support, she lifted the screen from its channel, maneuvered her screwdriver beneath it to release the latches, then set the whole framing on the ground. Maybe the judge was right, she told herself with a grin; this housebreaking business was child's play.

The window was stiff, sticking for an instant, but she pushed it upward. Setting the palms of her hands on the sill, Kelly boosted herself higher. Her block toppled from under her, falling to its side with a thud. She teetered for an instant, supporting herself with her arms. Then she grabbed for the inside molding of the window.

At a slight sound behind her, she hesitated, her nerves sounding a sudden alarm. Abruptly she was caught and dragged backward. She gave a cry of pain as her arm was scraped over the sill, and then she was dumped on her feet. Before she could move, before she could recover her breath, her wrist was snatched in an iron grasp and she was spun around.

"Who the hell are you, and what do you think you are doing?"

With those harsh words ringing in her ears, Kelly stared into the face of a tall, dark man. His black eyes burned with anger underscored by deadly menace. The chiseled lines of his features were implacable. His grip on her arm was so tight her hand was already turning numb. He wore only a brief white swimsuit, and the bronzed, muscled hardness of his body was jeweled with drops of water. There was about him the coiled strength, awaiting release, of a predator.

Shocked surprise held Kelly immobile for an instant, then fury came washing back along her veins in a warm rush. She jerked at her wrist, clasping her hand into a fist. "Let me go!"

Immediately her arm was twisted behind her back and she was brought up against the ridged firmness of the man's body. "I asked you two questions," he said, "and I suggest you come up with answers—fast!"

His voice was quieter, with a soft timbre that rasped along her nerves with the feel of sandpaper. There was also a faint foreign intonation in it, not quite an accent, and yet not wholly American despite his completely idiomatic phrases. He was, perhaps, in his early thirties. The black waves of his hair were sculpted to his head with dampness, and his brows, drawn together over piercing eyes, were thick and dark. Kelly felt the prickle of fright along her spine as she became intensely aware of the steely grasp that held her and the quick rise and fall of her breasts that were pressed against his chest so closely she could feel the imprint of

6

the gold medallion he wore on a chain around his neck. His grip tightened.

"I—I'm a family friend of the people who own this house," she said on a gasp, "and just who are you?"

She might as well not have spoken. "What do you think you're doing, sneaking around here?"

"I have a perfect right to be here, which is more than you can say!"

"What makes you think so?" he grated.

As his hold tightened inexorably, panic rose to her head. She began to kick and struggle, despite the strain on her twisted shoulder that made it feel as if it were coming out of the socket. Doubling the fist of her free hand as Mark and Peter had taught her one distant summer, she struck at his face, catching him in the mouth.

He swore under his breath, shifting his stance. Her other wrist was caught and pinioned behind her back also. Rage at her own helplessness rose in a red haze before her eyes. She lifted her gray gaze to his face, searching for some small sign of what he wanted, what he intended, dreading what she might find. He was so close she could see the gold flecks in the depths of his eyes, the sweep of his lashes, even the dark shading of his beard under his skin. On his bottom lip was a dark red spot of blood from the split place where she had hit him. A shudder ran over her, but she refused to look away.

Imperceptibly, his grasp loosened. "Why are you here?" he repeated.

She moistened her dry lips with the tip of her tongue. "An invitation."

"From whom?"

"Mary—Mary Kavanaugh, and her mother."

"And in order to take advantage of their hospitality, you had to crawl through a window?"

"The key wasn't where the judge used to keep it."

Anger at the sarcasm in his tone darkened her gray eyes once more.

"And that was?"

The inadvisability of answering such a question from a stranger flitted across her mind, but it seemed she had no choice. As his grip increased once more, she said, "Under—under the fern tub."

He held her gray gaze, his expression intent, measuring. Though a little of the tension seemed to leave him, it was still as though an electric current raced between them, passing wherever their bodies touched. His dark glance flicked over the pale oval of her face, coming to rest on her lips, pressed tight against the growing urge to plead with him to let her go.

"How did you get here?"

"I came in my car."

"Where is it?"

"Parked at the side of the house."

He looked away then, to where the back bumper of the small car could just be seen at the corner, though it would not be visible from the lake, the direction from which he had come. He gave what might have been a nod of satisfaction, then looked down at her once more, his gaze settling on the pulse that throbbed in her throat, then dropping to the curves of her breasts and shoulders outlined by the soft terry cloth. Tilting his head, he let his gaze run down over her brief shorts.

"It seems unlikely that you could be concealing a weapon," he drawled, "but it might be better to be safe than sorry."

By the time his meaning penetrated her haze of disbelief, it was over. He had released her wrist, and with quick and easy competence, run his hands over the curves and hollows of her body.

She stumbled back, trembling with rage and the need to strike out at him as her face flamed with color. What kept her from hitting him was the lack of feeling in her fingers, and the certain knowledge that retribution would be swift.

"Who do you think you are?" she cried.

"Who I am doesn't matter," he told her. "What concerns us at the moment is the fact that Judge Kavanaugh gave me permission to stay in his house. I have been here several days already, and intend to stay several more."

"Judge Kavanaugh told you—"

"He said I was to make myself at home, though he never mentioned sending a female along for companionship."

"He didn't!" Kelly said indignantly. "That is, I was told I could come, but nobody mentioned you being here, either—which seems a little strange!"

"Undoubtedly the judge neglected to inform his family," the dark man said, not at all discomfited by the hostile manner in which she was regarding him.

"That doesn't sound like Judge Kavanaugh to me."

It was true that things had been in an uproar at the Kavanaugh house with the preparations for going to Europe, and that Mrs. Kavanaugh could not be expected to have any great interest in the lake house after so many years. Still, the judge and his wife were a close couple who discussed everything except the most confidential aspects of his work. He must have mentioned such a matter as a guest at the lake house to her, if only to be certain that the place was fit for company.

"The fact remains that I am in residence, and have no intention of leaving. You will have to make other arrangements. I understand there is a fisherman's lodge on the other side of the lake. You should be able to find accommodation there."

His supreme self-confidence was daunting. It was possible, of course, that the judge had issued an invitation. If he hadn't been so rough, had not performed that last embarrassing search, she might have been inclined to leave and allow him possession of the place in peace. As it was, she did not feel so obliging.

"You have been here some time," she said. "Why can't you pack up and go to this lodge?"

"It doesn't suit me," he answered, his tone soft.

"Well, it doesn't suit me either." Kelly lifted her chin, silver lights flashing in her gray eyes.

He let his dark gaze drift down over her in insolent appreciation. "There's an easy solution. Stay here with me. There's plenty of bedrooms, not that we will need more than one."

"You—you—" There were no words to express her feelings without resorting to profanity.

His face tightened. "Take care," he said, an odd note in his voice that was at variance with the naked interest he allowed to surface in his eyes. "If we are going to spend any length of time together, it will be better if we don't get off on the wrong foot."

It was beginning to look as if the most intelligent thing she could do was to get away from the lake house while she still could. "We aren't! The only way I could be persuaded to spend time with you would be if I were roped and tied! I'm leaving, but I'm certainly going to mention you to Judge Kavanaugh to make sure he knows what kind of man he has staying at his house."

An expression that could have been regret flickered in his dark eyes and was gone. "That will be a little difficult, won't it, since he's not at home."

"He'll be back," Kelly answered, her tone scathing, "though I expect by then you'll be gone."

She swung away from him. She had not taken two steps before she discovered she had lost one of her sandals in the scuffle. That she had failed to notice the fact until now was an indication of how upset she had been. It lay on the ground under the window. With a hard look that dared him to comment, she bent to pick up her footwear.

Her attention was caught by the sound of voices. They came from the direction of the guest cottage that could barely be seen through the trees, on the opposite side of the house from where Kelly had parked. A moment later, two men appeared, coming along the overgrown path. The first was stooped and elderly with graying hair and gold-rimmed glasses. He was dressed casually in a pair of bright blue coveralls. Behind him was a hefty giant of a man whose balding head was fringed with black hair. He wore a white shirt buttoned to the collar, creased dress pants, and highly polished street shoes. Across his burly chest was strapped a black leather holster, and in it rested a heavy snub-nosed revolver.

The man beside Kelly swore a sibilant oath in what might have been the French language. At the sound, the two men looked up. With surprising quickness, the bigger of the two caught the arm of the elderly man and swung him around. With one hand on his gun, keeping a hard stare on Kelly, he pulled the other man back down the path with him, in the direction of the cottage.

What in the name of heaven was going on here? Kelly lowered her head and slipped on her sandal. With a fine pretense of oblivion, without daring to look at the man beside her, she turned toward her car.

"Wait."

"I—I can't stay, not if I'm going to find another place before it gets dark." She edged along another step or two, aware that he was moving after her.

"I think it might be better if you stayed here after all."

"I couldn't, really."

"I think you must."

"No!" As he reached out for her, she evaded his hand, sprinting for her car. She dived for the handle, but as she pulled the door open, it was slammed shut again. His hard fingers closed on her elbow.

"I insist," he said gently.

She twisted around to stare at him, her eyes wide. "You can't keep me here."

"Can't I?"

She fought him in silent fury then, kicking, clawing, using fists, knees, resisting with every ounce of will and strength. It did no good. He countered her blows, avoided her nails, held her until she tired, and then bending swiftly, caught her with one arm under the knees and lifted her high against his chest. Swinging her dizzyingly, he strode around toward the front of the house where it faced the lake.

He snatched open the screen door, shouldering through to the main entrance. Holding her with an iron grip, he reached for the knob and pushed inside. The front door had not even been locked. Before that fact had time to register, before her eyes were adjusted to the gloom after the brightness outside, Kelly was thrown down on a leather couch on her back. The man dropped down beside her, pinning her wrists to the leather with his hands on either side of her face.

With a strangled cry catching in her throat, she strained against him, writhing, trying to slide from the couch. He leaned over her, pressing her down with his weight until she was motionless.

"Lie still," he grated, his mouth inches from her ear. "I'm not going to rape you!"

She could hardly breathe, much less move. She lay rigid, allowing the words to sink in, aware of the steady beating of his heart against her and the pounding of the blood in her veins. By slow degrees, he raised himself from her, though he did not release her arms. Leaning over her on the couch, he surveyed her golden-brown tresses spread in a fan around her flushed face, and the panting rise and fall of her breasts. His black gaze fastened on the gray pools of her eyes, clouded now with the forced knowledge of her own vulnerability.

The sound of their breathing was loud in the quiet. Kelly lowered her lashes, concentrating on the shining gold disk that hung between them, swinging slowly from its chain around his neck.

"Who are you?" she asked, her voice a thread of sound.

"You may call me Charles. The last name doesn't matter."

"Why are you doing this?" The gleaming disk was a religious medal showing a relief of St. Michael, the patron saint of warriors.

"My reasons don't concern you."

The coolness of his tone touched her on the raw. "Don't concern me! How can they not concern me if you won't let me go?"

"Maybe," he said with deliberate irony, "I felt a sudden need for company."

"I don't believe it. Those two men—"

"Are good friends, but they are no substitute for a beautiful woman."

"You can't do this, you can't," she said, her voice rising as she lifted her gaze to his black eyes once more.

"It seems, my sweet, that I already have. Since we are going to spend some time together, I may as well know your name, too."

She compressed her lips, the look in her gray eyes defiant.

"I could call someone like you darling and dearest and sweetheart, but that might put me in an amorous mood. I don't *think* you would like that, though it's hard to be sure with women these days. We could experiment a little, by way of finding out."

His intention was plain as his glance flicked to her parted lips. She watched as he lowered his head, speculation lurking in the darkness of his gaze. A shiver ran over her nerves, and she tasted defeat. Against the firmness of his mouth as it hovered an infinitesimal space above hers she said, "Kelly. My name is Kelly."

Her strength was dissolving into a great lassitude. She grew aware of the heat of his body, of the corded muscles of his arms and shoulders, the board hardness of his chest with its furring of hair, and the flatness of his stomach above the low-riding waist of his swimsuit. Her own clothing was damp from the water that had been clinging to him, and as she watched, a drop of water edged from his hairline, running down the high ridge of his cheekbone.

"Who are you, Kelly?" he asked, his tone softly menacing, his breath warm against her lips.

Her eyes flew wide. "I told you."

"The only trouble is, I don't believe you. It's too much of a coincidence for me to swallow. I don't know how you found out where the key was kept, or who sent you, but I mean to learn before I let you go."

"Why? Why are you hiding here in the judge's house? If you weren't some kind of criminal it wouldn't make any difference who I am, or why I came. If you weren't some kind of a kidnapper or blackmailer, it wouldn't matter."

"Very clever," he murmured, his eyes narrowing.

"I saw the way your so-called friend with the gun hustled that old man out of sight," she went on, committing herself recklessly in her need to prevent him from carrying out his threat. "You found out the judge was out of the country, and you thought this would be a safe place to hide out, to keep a man prisoner while you waited for the ransom or—or something."

"You've got it all figured out, haven't you?" he said, his mouth brushing hers with a feathery touch that sent the quiver of something like excitement through her.

Kelly gave a reluctant nod.

"You understand then why I can't let you get away from me to go running to the police?"

She had expected him to deny it, to offer some explanation. There had been a moment when he had stiffened as if surprised, even angered, by the charge. His words of admission were smooth and easy, too easy, and always there was that lingering speculation in the watchful darkness of his eyes.

"Kelly?" The word was a threat.

"Yes," she said shortly, "I understand."

"Quite the little actress, aren't you? But it won't work. Who sent you here? Who knows where I am?"

"Nobody sent me. I came because it was my vacation and Mary Kavanaugh and her mother offered the house to me. It's the truth!"

The words were smothered against her lips as his mouth took hers with bruising force. Searing in its contempt, it was a kiss that promised greater violation. Kelly tasted the saltiness of blood from the cut on his lip, tasted too the humiliation of the enforced intimacy. As she felt the probing of his tongue, she turned her head sharply. He gave a moment's attention to the sensitive corner of her mouth, then trailed a path of fiery kisses along the curve of her cheek to the tender hollow of her throat. With tantalizing slowness, he dropped lower, to the beginning of the valley between her breasts just above the scooped neckline of her cotton terry top.

"Who sent you?" he queried, his tone low and husky.

"I—I told you. I can't help it if you won't believe me."

At the tremor of tears in her voice, he raised his head, drawing back to study the silvery shimmer of her eyes. Kelly lowered her lashes in an instinctive protective gesture, an unaccountable ache in her throat.

From the direction of the screen door beyond the veranda there came a knock. So on edge were Kelly's nerves that she started, her gaze swinging toward the sound. The shadowy figure of the man with the holstered gun could be seen through the front door that stood open.

"Saved," the man who had called himself Charles said, glancing from the man who waited to Kelly, his black gaze mocking as he released her and got to his feet. "One of us, at least."

❈ Chapter 2 ❈

The murmur of voices came from the steps beyond the screening of the veranda. Charles and the other man had stepped away from the house a few paces so as not to be overheard. Kelly swung her feet off the couch and sat up. She would not be lying there when Charles got back. In fact, if she were extremely careful, she might not be there at all.

The front door was still open. She could see the two men through it, but could they see her in the darker interior of the house? It was difficult to be certain, yet they did not glance in her direction as she got to her feet and moved deeper into the room, toward the kitchen area.

The living area of the house was a large, open space lined with the soft sheen of pine paneling or built-in bookcases, and shaped like an inverted letter L. The kitchen was in the shorter portion, with the dining area between it and the living room where the couch sat. There was a second outside door which opened from the kitchen onto the veranda that enclosed the house on three sides. If she could make it that far unseen, she might be able to ease out this side door, and then from the veranda reach the place where her car was parked.

17

The car was not visible from where Charles stood, but she could be certain the slightest noise would alert him to what she was doing. Holding onto the back of a chair, Kelly slipped out of her sandals, leaving them lying beside it. Her feet bare, she glided noiselessly and with slow care through the dining area, skirting the table. She touched the island cabinet that divided the dining alcove from the kitchen as she passed it, then came to a halt. The cabinets, the sink, and the electric range were surprisingly clean, all things considered. She did not have time to wonder at it, however. Barely breathing, she ghosted to the outside door. She flipped the lock, then closing her hand around the knob, turned it with exquisite care. Drawing the panel open, she slipped through, then stood listening. She could still hear the deep voices of the two men.

Resisting the urge to make a dash for the car, she edged across the veranda and pushed open the screen. It creaked on rusty hinges, a deafening sound. Kelly froze. The seconds ticked past. She could no longer hear Charles's voice, but no one came. Taking a deep breath, she moved down the steps and crossed the open space to her car. As quietly as possible, she released the door latch and slide inside. She would not slam the door shut until she had started the engine. She reached for the key.

It was not there. The ring with the ignition key was gone. She bent to search the floorboard, knowing all the time that she had not removed it. With a sinking feeling in the pit of her stomach, she sat up, scanning the seat, reaching for her shoulder bag which lay next to her.

"Is this what you are looking for?"

She swung sharply on an indrawn breath. Charles stood leaning on the top of the open car door, her keys dangling from his fingers just above her head. She could not prevent herself from snatching at them. Instantly, they were jerked out of her reach.

18

"I took the liberty of removing them while you were creeping about in the dining room and kitchen. You must take me for an idiot to think you could get away so easily."

She clenched her teeth with the rage that gripped her, her thoughts too incoherent for her to form words, to express how she felt.

"Get out," he said, the words a quiet command.

"What I take you for," she said, finding her tongue, "is a petty crook, a sneaking, vicious hoodlum who should be in jail!"

His eyes took on the hard glaze of obsidian and a shading of color receded from under the bronze of his skin as he answered, "Not petty, or you would never have been allowed to finish that little speech. Are you going to come out of there, or am I going to have to drag you out?"

Cooperating with him in any way was galling, but the danger in allowing him to put his hands on her again was too great to risk. She stepped from the car and stood facing him, her gray eyes smoldering.

"In the house." He jerked his head toward the side door, and when she had moved aside, slammed the car door shut behind her.

As he swung toward her, Kelly took a hurried step away from him. Her bare foot came down on something sharp and piercing. The next instant, that small pain was forgotten as Charles took her arm, marching her ahead of him up the steps and across the veranda into the kitchen.

He did not stop there, but guided her through the dining room and down the hallway that branched off toward the bedrooms. At the door of the first one on the right, he stopped. As he pushed the panel open, Kelly wrenched her arm from his grasp, backing away from him.

"You do place a high value on your virtue, don't

you?" he said, one eyebrow lifted as he regarded her in the dimness of the hall.

"And a low value on your word," she returned, her gray gaze steady.

She saw him tense, like an animal ready to spring, saw his face harden. A muscle corded in his jaw, then abruptly he relaxed, giving a short nod.

"I want to put on some clothes," he said, "and while I'm doing it, I want you in my sight. We can do this the easy way, or you can make it hard on yourself; either way, you are going into this room with me."

Kelly stared at him as he stood holding the door. For some reason that she could not explain, she felt that he meant exactly what he said, no more and no less. She also sensed that if she fought him the outcome might not be so cut and dried. Forcing her stiff limbs to take the necessary step toward him was one of the most difficult things she had ever done. He stood unmoving as she brushed past him into the bedroom, then as she came to a halt in the middle of the floor, he entered behind her, going to where a pair of brown pants and a cream-colored polo shirt lay across the foot of the bed.

She stared out the window that opened onto the front veranda, her gaze on the narrow stretch of the lake that could just be seen between the trees. Even so, she was intensely aware of him stepping into his pants, pulling them up over his swimsuit with swift, economical movements. He shrugged his shirt on over his head, and stepped into the connecting bath to towel his hair dry. Combing it with his fingers, he searched out a pair of tennis shoes and slipped them on. She flung him a quick glance as he picked up a flat gold watch from the bedside table and strapped it on his wrist.

Moving to the door once more, he made her a mocking bow. "After you."

In the hall he paused to flick the dial of a wall thermostat. Immediately the air conditioning unit came on, blowing cool air through the house. As they passed on into the living area, he moved to shut the door in the kitchen and also the front door, closing out the stifling heat of the waning day, closing them in together.

"Would you care for something cool to drink?" he inquired, his tone polite.

"No, thank you."

He sent her a long glance, then moved to the kitchen cabinet, taking down two glasses. Removing ice from the refrigerator, he dropped it clinking into the heavy tumblers, then opened a bottle of cola, filling them to the rim. Striding to the table, he set the glasses down with a thump. He pulled out a chair, resting his hands on the back. His black gaze hard, he said, "Sit down."

"I would rather stand," she answered mutinously.

"For how long? You are going to be here for some time, of that much I can assure you."

Kelly flicked a quick look at the chair, feeling suddenly drained and weary. Pitting her will against his over such a small matter was useless. She would do better to save her strength for more important issues. Pressing her lips together, avoiding his eyes, she moved to slide onto the chair he offered.

There was a strained moment when he stood stiff and silent behind her. Kelly thought she could feel the heat of his gaze traveling over her hair and shoulders, then he swung away, moving to take his seat across the table from her.

He took a long swallow of his drink, then set the glass back down. His dark regard rested on her slim fingers as she toyed with the frosted sides of her glass, then moved upward along her arms and shoulders to the faint flush of color that lay across her cheekbones before returning once more to her hands.

"You don't wear a ring of any kind. Does that mean there's no husband, no fiancé, no boyfriend close enough to give you one of those sentimental little promise rings?"

21

"The state of my love-life is none of your business," she snapped, flashing him a look of scorn.

"I take that to mean there isn't, since I don't doubt for a minute that you would have dragged him forward as a form of protection, if nothing else."

His acuteness making her voice grim, she said, "Think what you like."

"You mentioned a vacation; your first job?"

"What of it?"

"Nothing," he answered smoothly. "I'm just curious."

"Curious like a fox." He was trying to see if she could keep her story straight, testing his impression of her.

"Should I be flattered?" he asked.

"If it suits you."

"It doesn't." he answered, his tone hardening. "What kind of job?"

"Secretary for a construction company, if you must know."

"How long have you known the judge and his family?"

"What does it matter?" Since she had been expecting something of the sort, the change of subject did not throw her off balance.

"I asked you a question and, if you will remember, I like answers."

She sent him a look of purest dislike bordering on hate. "I have known them most of my life."

"Your mother and father are friends of theirs also, in fact?"

"My mother and father are dead."

"Poor little orphan, all alone in the world. I suppose you live by yourself."

Kelly opened her mouth to give him a sharp answer when something in his expression warned her. He was trying to make her angry, trying to make her answer without considering the consequences. "You—would like to think so, wouldn't you? It would make it so much easier for you if there were no one to miss me if I didn't turn up in a day or two."

"Is there?" If he was disconcerted by her perspicacity, he gave no sign.

"Of course there is!"

"You were bound to say so. Who?"

"My landlady, my boss, the girls in the office where I work."

"All of whom know you left on vacation, and if they are aware that you came down here at all, must expect you to stay several days. I would be surprised if anyone starts to worry about you before next weekend, if then. And that will be long enough."

A tight feeling closed over Kelly's heart. "What— what do you mean?"

A smile curved his mouth, but did not light the darkness of his eyes. "It will be long enough for us to get to know each other, something I look forward to with—great anticipation."

Blindly, she reached out to pick up the drink he had poured for her, swallowing quickly against the dryness of her mouth. She doubted that his glib explanation was a true answer to her question, but if it had been made to reassure her, it had not succeeded.

Charles leaned back in his chair, his arm resting on the table in a deceptively relaxed pose. "I don't understand why you aren't married, or engaged at the very least. You are much too attractive to be running around free."

"Running around free, as you put it, is the way I like it. I don't have time for men."

"A liberated woman?"

"To the extent that I have my own living to make and no ties to hold me down, yes."

"That isn't what I meant, and you know it, though I won't press you. Why don't you get married and let some man take care of you?"

"The men I have met aren't interested in marriage."

"They prefer to play house? What can you expect of hard-hatted construction workers?"

"I have gone out with an architect or two, and an executive in a loan company. They weren't so different." The derision in her eyes was veiled by her lashes as she played with the ice in her glass, making it swirl around the side.

"They need to have their heads examined," he said.

She looked up quickly, her surprise mirrored in her gray eyes. She was in time to catch the scowl that crossed his face before he schooled his features to blandness. "I mean," he went on, as the memory of his threatening invitation hovered between them, "that their technique must have been all wrong."

"Yours is better?" she asked, her tone laced with acid.

"We'll have to see, won't we? Of course, if all else fails, I can always fall back on force."

"That is exactly what I was getting at," Kelly flung at him, the flush of embarrassed fury creeping under her skin.

"A pity. For a minute I thought you might be interested in a comparison."

"You thought no such thing!"

"A man can dream, can't he?"

Kelly stopped, disconcerted. For an instant there had been a flash of real laughter lighting his eyes with warmth and enjoyment. Then the mocking challenge had closed over his face once more, igniting her urge to hit out at him. Never in her life had she felt such a need for physical retaliation. In some dim recess of her mind, she was shocked at the violence that shook her, causing the foundations of her quiet and tranquil personality to tremble with this wild need to join battle with the man across the table from her, and with the equally strong counter-instinct that warned her she could not win.

"You have an expressive face," he said, irony strong in his voice.

Kelly looked away from him. Beyond the windows and the screened veranda, the sun was setting, its long rays slanting through the trees with crimson light, turning the waters of the lake to an iridescent, rose-tinted, blackish green. On its still surface were reflected the stretching shadows of the trees, the stately cypresses mired knee-deep in the muddy lake, their feathery branches like arms uplifted in supplication. A blue heron flapped across the open space in arrow-straight flight, the dark underside of its wings flushed with pink. On the distant horizon of the opposite shore, the trees that lined it were already black with the approach of night.

Kelly dropped her hands into her lap, clenching them together. She took a deep breath. As if compelled, she said, "What do you intend to do with me?"

"Why belabor the point?" he asked after a long moment.

"Because I have to know!" she cried, swinging to face him. "You have no right to keep me here, no right to interfere with my life! I want to know why you're doing it."

"Can't you just accept it? Can't you relax and take things as they come?"

"Could you?" she demanded.

"I'm not a woman."

"That has nothing to do with it! It makes it worse, if anything!" She lifted her small fist and brought it down on the table with a bang.

"Kelly—" There was a warning note in his voice. He reached across the table to place his strong fingers on her arm.

She shook off his hand, coming up out of her chair so quickly it toppled over behind her. As he surged upward, rounding the table toward her, she retreated. Suddenly he came to a halt. He straightened, a stillness coming over him. Watching him, Kelly realized how dim it was growing in the room. His face was in shadow, the features unreadable.

"Kelly, wait," he said, his voice soft. "I don't want to hurt you; I won't, unless you force me."

His voice with its promise of a modicum of safety was hypnotic. She wanted to believe him, needed to believe him. She could feel the tight coil of her resistance beginning to unwind. This new attack upon her defenses might well prove to be more dangerous than physical force.

"Behave myself like a good little girl, is that it?" she lashed out at him. "You would like that, wouldn't you? It would make things so much easier for you!"

"It might well be that I would prefer it not to be easy." His voice was quiet, almost reflective.

"You should be happy then," she said with a lift of her chin, "because I intend to make it as difficult for you as I can."

The steady hum of the cooling system was loud in the silence that stretched between them. With an exclamation under his breath, he swung away from her. Striding to the light switch, he flipped it on. As the room sprang into bright detail, he stood staring around him with his hands on his hips and a grim look on his face.

"This house," he said with measured emphasis, "has too many doors and windows."

Kelly tilted her head to one side. "What a shame."

"It means I will have to keep a close eye on you, stick to you day and night like the proverbial leech."

Day and night. She swallowed, her inclination to bait him rapidly disappearing. "How—exhausting."

"Possibly, though it may have its compensations."

"Not," she said with more bravado than she felt, "if I can help it."

"Yes, but can you?" he queried softly.

Their eyes met across the width of the room, clear

gray clashing with opaque black. What was he trying to do, frighten her into submission? If so, it was entirely possible he might succeed. And yet, there was an odd kind of courage to be gained from the reflection that if he wanted to subdue her completely, he had only to use those tools of the kidnapper's trade, the gag and bonds. She would give him a fierce run for his money, of course, but she had felt enough of his strength to have little doubt as to the outcome. That he had not yet brought them out was a source of wonder, and puzzlement.

"I can try," she said, and was disgusted with herself when the words left her throat as no more than a whisper.

With the beginning of a frown between his eyes, he moved away from her. He stopped at the front window, staring out for a long moment with his back to the room. He made a movement with his shoulders that might have been a shrug, then reached to draw the drapes, shutting out the twilight.

"Can you cook?"

The prosaic nature of the question was so strange that it was a moment before Kelly could form a response. "Yes."

"Steak?"

"I'm not up to *cordon bleu* standards, but I can broil a cut of meat."

"Good. That should keep you occupied for a while."

"If you think I'm going to cook your dinner for you—"

"And your own, of course."

"Of course," she jeered, "and while I'm at it, why not enough for your friends in the guest cottage?"

"They can fend for themselves for the time being," he answered, his face impassive.

"Why? Don't you want the two prisoners to become too chummy?" she demanded.

"Maybe I would rather be alone with you," he told her, his voice silky.

"I don't want to be alone with you."

"You have made that abundantly clear. I hope I have made it just as plain that what you want doesn't matter?"

She longed to defy him, to tell him to cook his own dinner, but from the glint in his eyes, she thought that was just what he expected her to do. The hard fact of the matter was she was weak from hunger. She had been so busy packing that morning that she had taken time for only the sketchiest breakfast and had skipped lunch entirely. She had thought to stop for a sandwich on the way, but she had forgotten how scarce were fast-food places on the back roads that led to the lake. The mere thought of a steak, and perhaps a salad, was enough to make her mouth water. What good was all her righteous anger if she lacked the strength to sustain it? How could she manage to escape if she was too weak to run?

That was not the only problem. As she swung on her heel, heading for the kitchen, she felt a sharp pain stab into her instep. There was something in her foot, probably a thorn from the locust trees in the surrounding woods. She would deal with it later, when she was alone, if she was permitted the luxury of privacy. For the moment, it only hurt if she stepped on it a certain way. If she took care, she should be able to get through the rest of the evening. With so much else to worry her, a thing as little as a thorn could be ignored.

If she had thought she was going to escape the watchful gaze of her captor, she was disabused of the notion in short order. Charles moved after her into the kitchen where he perched on a wooden stool beside the island cabinet in relaxed comfort, his dark eyes following her every movement.

With a fine pretense of indifference, Kelly took the steaks from the refrigerator and unwrapped them.

Switching on the broiler to let it begin heating, she took out the broiler pan, then opened a drawer and selected a sharp knife to score the fat and keep the steaks from curling. The kitchen was well stocked; it took her only a moment to assemble the salt, pepper, and butter. That done, she rummaged through the refrigerator once more to see if he had the makings of a salad. Finding lettuce and a tomato, she swung to the cabinet where Mrs. Kavanaugh had always kept the large plastic container she had used for tossing salad greens. It wasn't there.

"Is that what you're looking for?" Charles asked, nodding toward the top of the refrigerator.

He was using the container as a fruit bowl. Kelly glanced at the oranges and bananas it held, then took down a pair of individual salad bowls.

"I will have to admit you know your way around this kitchen," Charles said, his tone thoughtful.

She paused, her back to him. "Did you really think I wouldn't?"

"My mind is open on the subject."

"What earthly reason would I have for coming down here except the one I gave you?" Kelly removed the core of the lettuce, slicing around it with her knife, then tearing it out with a quick twist of her fingers before she ripped the head of iceberg apart, letting water run over it in the sink.

"Information?" he suggested.

"What do you mean? As some kind of police spy? That's ridiculous."

"You certainly don't look the part," he agreed, leaving his stool to come and stand beside her, reaching for a piece of crisp lettuce to crunch between his white teeth.

"That's something, anyway," Kelly snapped. Setting the lettuce aside to drain, she picked up the tomato and the knife.

"But then," he said meditatively, "it would be stupid

29

of them to send someone who obviously looked like—police."

She had the strange idea that he had substituted that last word for another he had started to use. She gave him a quick glance. "If you really thought I had that kind of connection you would be more worried. Supposing I were on a special assignment, someone would be expecting my report."

"That leaves you in a dilemma, doesn't it? Whether to try to convince me that you are, or that you aren't."

If she was with the police, then someone might come looking for her after a time. If not, he had no reason to distrust her, but also no reason to fear her superiors would send someone after her. Kelly turned to face him, her paring knife in her hand. "I only want you to see the truth, that I am no danger to you, that I have no interest in you or your friends."

He did not move, there was no outward sign, and yet she was aware of the alertness that galvanized him as she turned the blade of her knife in his direction. He leaned against the cabinet, his unprotected chest, with the polo shirt taut across its muscled width, only inches from her. If she made a movement toward him with the steel, would she ever reach him, or would swift counter-measures prevent her from making contact? The thought of using the sharp knife against him had not occurred to her until she sensed his guard against it. Why it hadn't, she could not tell; she should have been looking for weapons. Regardless, she had no stomach for the thought of slicing his flesh in such a way, even if the odds for success had been more favorable than they were.

Almost against her will, she raised her gray eyes to his dark and suspended stare. Turning the knife handle in his direction, she said, "You may as well do your share. You can cut up the tomatoes for the salad while I put on the steak."

He took the knife in one hand and the tomato in the

other. He still stood weighing her words, watching her, when she turned away.

They spoke little as they ate their meal and cleared away after it. Charles, with perfect aplomb, rinsed and dried the dishes as she washed them. Kelly tried to disregard his nearness, and also the distrust that made him determined to keep her within easy reach. It could not be done. Once their shoulders brushed as he leaned to pick up a cup at the same time she dropped a fork into the steaming rinse water. The contact sent a shock along her arm that she felt to the tips of her fingers. It suddenly seemed unreal, beyond belief that she could be where she was, alone in the lake house with a stranger, a ruthless man who was keeping her a prisoner, one who saw her as desirable and took great pains to make her aware of it. Darkly handsome, he moved back and forth in the small kitchen with lithe, catlike grace. And beyond the drapery-covered windows, the night drew in, advancing with ponderous slowness toward the time when they would have to go to bed.

As if attuned to her thoughts, Charles spoke. "Do you have anything outside in your car that you might need tonight?"

She flicked him a wary glance, discarding the impulse to ask him one more time to let her go. "My suitcase, I suppose, and there is an ice chest with a few things in it that should be put in the refrigerator."

"If you will point them out, I will bring them in for you." His offer was politely helpful, with no hint of the unspoken demand that she stay in his sight.

Her back stiff with resentment, Kelly marched before him out to the car and stood to one side while he inserted the key and lifted the trunk lid. In careful monosyllables, she indicated the things she wanted. Taking her canvas shoulder bag containing her billfold and cosmetics and a brown paper bag filled with paperback books from the front seat, she left him to struggle with the ice chest and her larger suitcase.

"You came prepared, didn't you?" he commented as he dumped the chest on the cabinet in the kitchen.

"I told you I meant to be here for a week."

"So you did." He sent her a tight glance, but if he found reason in her obvious preparations for a long stay to accept that she was no more and no less than what she had said, he was not ready to concede it.

"You wouldn't trust your own mother," she exclaimed, angry disappointment flaring in her eyes.

"We'll leave her out of this, if you don't mind." His tone was cool, but final.

"You mean you have a mother?" The words were out before she considered how they might sound, jarred from her by surprise at his protective attitude.

"Most people do," he answered dryly.

"I wonder—" she began, then stopped.

"You were saying?" he prompted, though there was a forbidding look in his face.

In a rush, she said. "I wonder what this mother of yours would think if she knew what you were doing now."

Amusement crossed his features and was gone. "She would shake her head in sorrow over her wayward son, and wonder at the wisdom of his running such a risk."

"I told you, I am no danger to you!"

"The picture of innocence, aren't you?" he said, then added cryptically, "I think that's what is bothering me."

Was the doubt he had expressed good or bad from her point of view? It was impossible to tell, impossible to decide what to say to help her case. Searching the grim mask of his face, Kelly made no reply.

He hefted her suitcase. "Come on," he said, "it's time I showed you where you are going to sleep."

She moved before him down the hall, edging gingerly past the first bedroom that he had made his own. She came to a halt automatically outside the room directly across the hall on the left, the one where she and Mary Kavanaugh had slept. Charles opened the door and looked in, then shook his head. Further along, he took a disparaging inventory of the next bedroom on the back side of the house, then moved purposely back across the hall to the other front bedroom, the one beside his own.

"This will do. You have a view of the lake and your own bath." His voice dropping to a quieter note, he went on. "But there is only a wall between us, and I am a very light sleeper. If you walk across the floor or open a window, I will hear you. If you turn in your sleep, you will wake me. This should be sufficient warning for you not to try anything during the night. If you do, I can promise you that your next sleeping arrangement will not be as spacious, or as private."

He meant, in short, that he would force her to share his room, if not his bed. As incensed as she was with the threat beneath his words, she still had the presense of mind to be relieved. Caught between those warring emotions, she could think of nothing to say. Her face stony, she watched as he set down her suitcase, then pointedly leaving the door wide open, took himself out of the room.

✤ Chapter 3 ✤

Kelly placed her shoulder bag on the bedside table, put her bag of books beside it, then dropped down on the bed. Closing her eyes, she released her breath in a soundless sigh. She lifted her shoulders, feeling the tenseness of the muscles of her neck from the strain of the past hours. What was she going to do? The situation was intolerable, but try as she might, she could see no way out. She was trapped, a captive at the mercy of the enigmatic man who called himself Charles.

For a time, she had thought mercy was something the man who held her lacked. There had been nothing in his reception to encourage her to expect it. Thinking back, it seemed that his first suggestive remarks had been made with the idea of speeding her departure. They had been most effective; she had been more than ready to leave when she had caught sight of the elderly man and his gun-carrying guard.

She had not been meant to see those two; that much was plain. The fact that she had was the reason she was being kept here against her will, the reason Charles had used such drastic measures to extract the information he wanted from her.

Would he have carried through his threats of physi-

34

cal intimacy? Would he still do so if she defied him? She did not know. It seemed probable, and yet, he had been extremely considerate over the sleeping arrangements. Moreover, there had been a short time when he had dropped his menacing attitude, becoming almost human. It was difficult to know what to make of him. Her thoughts and emotions were in chaos, impossible to sort out. The evidence of her own eyes convinced her that there was something sinister involved here, and that Charles, if he was not behind it, was at least deeply committed to it. She was suspicious of him, she distrusted him, and if she were honest, she would have to acknowledge that she was afraid of him. Still, she could not forget the burgeoning excitement she had felt when he held her, or the tumult of the senses she had endured during his kiss. Her reactions were disturbing. To think that she had no more control than that over her bodily responses filled her with distress. The only thing that gave her comfort was the thought that she had not revealed her humiliating weakness to Charles.

Raising her head, she looked around the room. It was large and airy with double windows on the front and side, both sets of which opened onto the veranda. They were covered with drapes in a cool green-and-white bamboo pattern. A matching spread was draped over the bed with its headboard of rattan. Dark green rugs were scattered here and there over the polished floors. The accent color in the room was bright yellow, brought out in a lamp base made from a ginger jar, and a set of bird prints framed in yellow bamboo against the stark white walls. Overhead was a ceiling fan slowly revolving to stir the cool air. The turning blades cast shadows on the walls, making a rhythmic, beating sound that was oddly soothing, and might well drown out a little of the sound of her movements.

She could not depend on it. With a weary shrug, Kelly got to her feet, moving to where her suitcase sat on a wicker bench at the foot of the bed. Snapping the latches, she opened the case out flat and took from it a long gown of soft nylon in a pale green shade. She would not unpack. Surely by tomorrow something would happen, some change would take place so she could leave the lake house.

There was a lock on the bathroom door. She turned it with a decisive snap and immediately felt better. Running a deep tub of warm water, she dropped in a handful of herbal-scented bath beads, removed her clothes, and stepped in. For a long time she lay soaking, feeling the tension ease from her. It was only as she heard footsteps in the hall, pausing outside her bedroom door, that she roused herself to make splashing noises. The last thing she wanted was to remain so quiet that Charles would come pounding on the door, demanding that she show herself.

Her nightgown, with its heart-shaped neckline and front lacing like an Elizabethan basque, was more revealing than she had remembered. With her lips pressed tightly together, she sought out the negligee that went with it as a cover-up, but since the neckline of the negligee followed that of the gown, she was little better off. She glanced at the open door, a shadow in her gray eyes. Charles had gone, but she had no way of knowing when he might look in on her again. She was probably being ridiculous to think that the sight of her would inflame the man in the next room with desire. All his threats and insinuations to the contrary, he had most likely felt nothing whatever for her. It had been a game to insure her cooperation. That was all.

She thumbed through the books she had brought, selecting one of her favorite Regency novels. Settling in bed, propped on pillows against the headboard, she opened the book and started to read. She turned the first page, a second, a third. Then, her mouth set in a grim line, she read the first page again. The words could not entice her; the sentences had no meaning.

She lowered her book and lay listening. From the

direction of the living room, she could hear the sound of a low-turned radio, or was it a stereo phonograph? What was he doing, her jailer? Was he prowling the house, wishing he had never set eyes on her? Was he deciding what he was going to do with her, deciding when he could set her free, if he could set her free?

He didn't seem like a crook. The thought came unbidden, but she allowed it to linger. She had never known a criminal before, it was true, and she supposed the best of them, those who went undetected, must be just like other people, nondescript men and women who went about their lives without drawing attention to themselves. It had to be admitted, however, that such a description did not fit Charles either.

What was he then? What legitimate reason could he possibly have for holding a person prisoner? Was he a policeman? Some kind of detective? If so, why hadn't he shown her his credentials? Why would he play along with her accusation that he was a criminal, even to the point of making sarcastic remarks about she herself being from the police?

Some other branch of the law then, the FBI or the CIA? The same caveat applied. As far as she was aware, the representatives of government agencies were scrupulous about identifying themselves, and he would have had nothing to fear from her in any case. If any agent suspected her of wrongdoing after finding her crawling in the window, if she posed a threat to some undercover operation, he had only to call in the local authorities and tell them to come and take her away. The likelihood of her being held captive and subjected to his type of harassment was nil.

No, she was going to have to accept the fact that this man Charles was operating outside the law, that he was a hoodlum who specialized in abductions, or worse still, some sort of hired killer. It was all too likely that earlier, when she had thought he was interrogating her to find out who might be concerned if she turned up missing, he had been trying to discover if there was anyone willing to pay ransom for her release!

Such thoughts were not pleasant company, yet they stayed with her long after she had flung down her book and turned out the light. They would not let her sleep, but kept her tossing and turning as the hours stretched one into the other.

Charles was right about one thing; it was possible to hear every movement in the echoing openness of the house. She knew when he returned to his room, knew when he showered. She sat up in bed then, and even flung back the cover. But she realized after a moment that by the time she had slipped on her clothing and eased into his room to find her car keys, he would more than likely be out of the bathroom again. The last thing she needed was for him to discover her in his bedroom.

Of course, it was possible that she could get away from the house on foot. It was at least a mile to the nearest dwelling of any kind, however, and there was no guarantee that it would be occupied. Most of the homes on the lake were summer places, used a few months out of the year, or else over the weekends. She could walk miles and knock on doors for hours without finding anyone in residence this late on a Sunday evening in September. Charles, it seemed, had chosen his hideaway well. Kelly lay back down, staring with wide and burning eyes into the darkness.

It was sometime later when she came awake from a fitful slumber. She lay still, disoriented, caught at the edge of a nightmare she could not remember. Then she realized it was no dream but reality. She sat up abruptly, coming fully alert. That movement sent a throbbing pain up her leg. Her foot; she had forgotten the thorn. It was no wonder, but who could have thought it would hurt like this?

Pushing herself higher in the bed, she reached to turn on the lamp. She brushed the covers to one side, then turned her foot so she could look at it. The thorn was a gray line under the skin of the most tender portion of her instep. The area around it was red and swollen, and there was a red streak running up over the top of her foot. It was infected; there could be little doubt of that. She applied gentle pressure with her thumbs, but it did no good. The thorn was embedded. It was going to have to come out, and to do the job she was going to need a needle.

She rummaged in her shoulder bag, searching for a straight pin, a safety pin, anything that might be pressed into use. There was nothing, nor was there anything in the dresser drawers that she slid quietly open and shut. The medicine chest in the bathroom held basic supplies, but nothing sharp.

Standing in the middle of the floor, she tried to think. Mrs. Kavanaugh had been a needlewoman, forever stitching at embroidery of some kind, whether it was petit point, cross-stitch, or crewel work. There had been a worn, wooden sewing box that she had used. It was always kept in a cabinet in the living room. If the judge's wife had not changed her habits and her pastime, Kelly should be able to find what she sought there.

All was quiet in the next room. The cooling system had come on, masking a little of the sound she had made. Scarcely breathing, moving with care, she left her room and limped along the hall. As she passed the room where Charles was sleeping, she could not resist the impulse to glance in at the door. In the dim glow cast by the lamp in her bedroom, she could just see his shape upon the bed, see the dark splotch of his hair against the pillow, the sheet cutting across his waist, and one long arm flung above his head.

The pieces of furniture in the living room were bulky shadows in the darkness. She did not dare turn on the overhead light; it might wake the man sleeping down the hall behind her. There was no real need for it, not if the sewing box was where it had always been kept. She could find it by touch if need be, then carry it back to her bedroom to sort out what she wanted.

The cabinet was actually the lower portion of the built-in bookcase that took up one wall of the living room. The hinged wooden box was where she expected it to be, on the bottom shelf. With a sense of triumph, she knelt and pulled it out. Switching the handle to her right hand, she got to her feet.

Without warning, a hard hand closed on her shoulder. Charles whirled her around and scooped her into his arms.

"You!" she exclaimed.

"Who else did you expect?" came the hard reply. He swung around, striding toward the hall.

"I didn't. I—Charles, no!" The last cry came as he shouldered into his bedroom.

"I did warn you." Reaching the bed, he dropped her upon its surface. The fall jarred the handle of the sewing box she still clutched in her fingers. It tumbled away from her as Charles put one knee on the mattress and threw himself down beside her. She tried to twist away from him, but he was lying on the skirt of her gown and negligee. He clamped a hand to her waist, pulling her back against him. He hovered above her there in the darkness, the muscles in his arm slowly tensing, and then his mouth came down upon hers.

With firm and warm sensuality, he tasted her lips, exploring the sweetness of their gentle curves and the nectared moistness of one corner, insidiously increasing the pressure of his kiss until they parted under his. It was at that moment Kelly realized she had not attempted to resist him past that first instinctive protest, realized the treachery of her burning mouth and leaping pulse. The shock of that recognition gave her extra strength as she jerked away from him. He lunged after her, and with that violent movement, the sewing box teetering on the foot of the bed tumbled to the floor with a crash that sent buttons and bobbins, embroidery hoops and spools of thread scattering in every direction, skittering over the polished floor.

He went still, then with an oath, he sat up and turned on the light. His dark gaze moved from the debris on the floor to Kelly's flushed face as she lay beside him.

"What," he said with an expressive gesture, "are you doing creeping around in the dark with that thing clutched to your bosom?"

Kelly scrambled away from him, snatching her gown from under his thigh. "I wasn't creeping anywhere," she snapped. "I was taking the box back to my room to find a needle."

"Don't tell me, let me guess. You were overtaken in the night by a sudden urge to sew a seam?"

"I have," she informed him, her gray eyes stormy, "a thorn in my foot!"

He stared at her, his dark gaze moving slowly from the tumbled glory of her golden-brown hair to the rose-petal color on her cheekbones and the creamy softness of her shoulders, more revealed than concealed by the pale green garment she was wearing. A muscle corded in his jaw as he transferred his regard to the slim feet that were tucked under her as she hesitated, ready for flight.

"Let me see."

"I will not!" she returned, sliding from the bed, uncaring that her gown rode up well above her knees. She put her feet on the floor, and immediately winced.

He came up from the bed, a tall bronzed figure wearing only the bottoms to a pair of blue silk pajamas, outlined in a golden nimbus from the lamplight behind him. "I want to look at this thorn that's giving you so much trouble you had to rid yourself of it before dawn. If I have to do it the hard way, I will, but I would rather not be forced into it."

"It's no business of yours."

"If you think I'm going to let you neglect it to the point where I'll have to take you to a hospital, then you are mistaken."

"I never intended any such thing! It's just a thorn. I can tend to it myself!"

"How can I believe you, when you won't let me see?"

She had the feeling once more that she was being manipulated, but there seemed nothing she could do about it. There was about him that animal alertness, the assured confidence amounting to arrogance that told her it was useless to attempt to evade him. "Oh, all right!"

She sat down on the bed with a flounce. Lifting her gown, she crossed her ankle on her knee, turning the sole of her foot to the light. He went to one knee on the floor beside her, his fingers warm and gentle as they probed her instep.

"Um-hum," he said. Straightening, he moved into the bathroom, returning in a moment with a bottle of alcohol, a tube of ointment, and a collection of bandaging material. He placed these on the bedside table, then scanned the contents of the sewing box strewn over the floor. Kelly saw the gleam of the needle at the same time he did, but it was Charles who came up with it.

Without looking at her, he stepped to the bedside table, opened the bottle of alcohol, and plunged the needle into the contents. As he turned toward her once more, Kelly held out her hand.

He shook his head. "Turn over on your stomach."

"What?" She stared at him, her gray eyes wide.

"Roll over and put your foot on my knee. I can reach it better that way, and you won't have to watch what I'm doing."

"You are not going to do anything," she told him.

"But I am," he said softly.

"Why?" The word was bald, stiff with suspicion.

42

"A number of reasons. First of all, to see that it gets done properly. Second, because I can see the thing and get to it better than you can if you have to twist your ankle in your lap. And third, because—because I want to do it."

"I know. You will enjoy sticking a needle in me and watching me squirm!"

Anger leaped into his eyes. "No! Because I—" He pulled himself up short. When he spoke again, all expression was gone from his face. "I can hold you down, if you insist."

"If I insist? You must be crazy. All I want is to be left alone."

"The last thing that is likely to happen. Will you lie down?"

"I despise you!" she said, the words bursting from her before she could stop them.

"I don't doubt it. On your stomach, please."

The nagging pain in her foot exacerbated her nerves that were by no means calm in the first place. She wanted the thorn out, and the sooner the better. Just now, her swollen instep was a handicap that she could not afford if she meant to get into a foot race. And if she were caught and dragged struggling back to his bed, what would be the result of their tussles in their skimpy nightwear if he carried out his intention of forcing her to lie still under him? She had already had more than one demonstration of the chemistry that could be ignited between them. It would be foolhardy in the extreme to invite another.

Giving him a look of fulminating rage, Kelly stretched out face down across Charles's bed and buried her face in her arms. He sat down beside her, and picking up her ankle, set her foot on his knee directly under the light.

"I'm not going to hurt you," he said.

"It's a little late to worry about that, don't you think?" she said, her voice muffled.

"Such a martyr," he jeered. "I wonder if you will put yourself in your husband's hands so reluctantly and fatalistically on your wedding night."

"I hardly expect it to be the same as having a thorn removed," she said, her voice tart. Then, as the possible implications of her remark struck her, she was fervently glad that her face was hidden.

A tremor shook him, as of silent laughter. His tone suspiciously grave, he said, "I hope not."

The touch of his hands was firm, yet gentle, the restraint he kept on her movement complete. She felt the pricking of the needle against the tightly held skin of her instep. A shiver ran over her as the steel of the needle touched the thorn.

"It's deep," he said. "I can't think why in the name of heaven you didn't mention it earlier."

She unclenched her gritted teeth enough to say, "You were so busy threatening me, I couldn't get a word in edgewise."

"If I remember correctly, you did your share of the talking."

"For what good it did me."

He made no direct reply, asking instead, "When was your last tetanus shot?"

"What difference does that make?"

"It's a puncture wound, and this is cattle country. It's been against the law for several years to allow cattle to range free, but sometimes the farmers let them out in the winter."

"That's trusting of them, beef prices being what they are."

"Isn't it?" he said. "It also increases the danger of tetanus, if you take my meaning."

He was speaking of the germ's preference for incubation in fresh manure. She grimaced. "What would you say if I told you I had not had a tetanus vaccination since I was twelve?"

44

"I would send to the nearest hospital for serum and give it to you myself."

She didn't doubt it for a minute. His words, spoken without haste, were too even, too deliberate. "That won't be necessary. I had a booster when I went in for my physical before I started to work."

He gave a grunt of satisfaction, though whether it was for the information she had given him, or for the success of his operation, she could not tell. Hard on the sound, he said, "Here is what was causing your problem."

She lifted her head, twisting to see the prize. Nearly an inch long, it was a brownish-black locust thorn. She had hardly been aware of his deeper probing for it. She knew that she had the firmness of his grip around the point of entry to thank for that oblivion, and also his provocative comments that had distracted her, keeping her attention from what he was doing. She levered herself higher, trying to turn.

"Lie still."

She felt the sting and smelled the pungency of iodine, followed immediately by a soothing application of ointment. Over this he placed a square of sterile white gauze, then fastened it with strips of nylon tape. His movements were quick and sure, as if he knew exactly what he was doing.

"You go about that like a professional," she said, a tentative note in her voice.

"On a place as big as—" he began, then stopped, all expression leaving his face. "Let's just say I have had a little experience."

What had he been going to say? She could make no sense of it. "I suppose I should be grateful for it."

He did not answer. Kelly lowered her lashes as she realized how ungracious her comment sounded. Turning over, she sat up, pushing toward the edge of the bed.

"Not so fast," he said. Turning from tightening the

lid on the iodine bottle, he leaned to put one arm under her knees and the other across her back before he surged to his feet.

"I can walk," she protested as she found herself in his arms once more.

"Yes, but not run. You don't know how relieved that makes me."

"I can imagine," she said, though there was a shadow of nervousness in her eyes as he carried her from the room and down the hall.

"Can you?" he asked, "and are you also able to imagine what I am thinking now?"

"I prefer not to try."

"Wise girl," he said with a hint of self-mockery edging his tone.

He deposited her on the bed, then walked into the bathroom, returning a moment later with a tumbler of water and two white tablets. As he held the medicine out to her in the palm of his hand, Kelly eyed it skeptically.

"What is that?"

"Aspirin, nothing more I assure you."

"I don't need it." She sat where he had left her. She had pulled the sheet up to her waist, but she could not bring herself to lie back and relax.

"Do you feel you have to object to everything I say and do as a matter of principle, or do you just enjoy being stubborn?"

"It isn't being stubborn to object to being drugged!"

"If I wanted to put you out," he said, his black eyes holding the glint of steel, "I think I could find something stronger to push down your throat than two aspirin. Come on, they will help you sleep instead of lying here feeling sorry for yourself, or stomping up and down the hall keeping me awake."

"I should have known it was your comfort you were worried about," she flung at him.

"So you should. Why would I care about yours, after all?"

"No reason in the world, any more than I care whether you get your rest or not. It seems to me that you are the stubborn one, determined to force your will on me. What are you afraid of—that if you let me get around you in this one small thing, I may be able to do it with something more important?"

He stood looking down at her a long moment, the muscles standing out in the hard, bronzed planes of his face. Then abruptly he stepped to the bedside table where he set the glass down with a thud and placed the aspirins beside it.

"Take them or not, as you please," he said quietly, "but let me hear no more out of you until morning, or I refuse to be responsible for what happens!"

❋ Chapter 4 ❋

The aroma of coffee drifted into Kelly's dreams. It was a welcome morning smell. She stretched and opened her eyes. Her gray gaze focused on the ceiling fan twirling gently above her. She felt rested, surprisingly so. There was a twinge of soreness in her foot, but she did not think it was going to give her any trouble. The events of the night before flashed through her mind, and she closed her eyes. Charles had been right, damn him. The aspirin had helped, though she would die before she would tell him so.

He must be up, if there was coffee brewing already. It was strange, but the aspirins must have been a better restorative than she had thought. She felt well and able to join battle with him again this morning. She wasn't eager for it, of course. That would be expecting too much, even of such powerful medicine.

She turned her head, listening. The house was quiet. She could hear no sound of him moving about in the kitchen. She knew he could be extremely quiet when it suited his purpose, but surely there should have been some noise. Maybe he had gone outside. He might even have risen early for a swim.

It was then she saw the steaming cup of coffee. It sat

48

on her bedside table in the exact spot where the night before Charles had left the tumbler and tablets.

Fury rushed over Kelly, and she sat up. He had been here in her room this morning. He knew already that she had taken his blasted aspirins; there was no way she could keep the information from him. He had strolled in here while she slept as if he had a perfect right to enter her room, as if he owned the house and everything in it, master of all he surveyed. And what he had been surveying was her as she lay deep in slumber, unconscious, unaware.

Coffee! She longed to take the cup and throw it against the far wall. She reached out and picked it up, then as she smelled the delicious brew, the sacrifice seemed too great. She would drink his coffee, then she would get dressed and go find him for the express purpose of telling him what she thought of him. Talk about her sneaking and creeping around!

She pulled on a shorts outfit of crisp turquoise linen that gave her eyes a reflection of blue. Running a brush through her hair, she tied it back for coolness with a length of turquoise ribbon. Discarding the idea of footwear of any kind, she left her room with a militant set of her features.

The thermostat for the air conditioning had been switched off and the doors thrown wide to take advantage of the early-morning freshness. As she stopped just inside the living room, Kelly glanced out through the front entrance. Charles was there, standing in front of the house beyond the screened veranda, in close conversation once more with the person who had been guarding the elderly man. With their backs to the house, they looked out over the lake as they spoke. The murmur of their voices came to Kelly where she stood, though she could not distinguish the words.

Almost without thinking, she edged toward the veranda, favoring her injured foot as she quickly crossed the open doorway, using the cover of the front wall to conceal her stealthy approach. Flattening her back against the paneling, she held her breath to listen.

The man with the revolver was speaking. "Seeing that girl yesterday really upset the old guy, made him think about how long it's been since he saw his own family. He hasn't given me too much trouble, you know, not since the first day or two, but he was sure restless this morning."

"It won't be too long now," Charles said.

"We hope. Could drag on for months yet."

"I don't think so," Charles returned. "I believe the payoff will come in a week, two at the most."

Kelly clamped her hand over her mouth to prevent her gasp of consternation. She had been right; they were holding the old man she had seen for ransom.

"If he's still alive by that time."

"Yes," Charles said, his tone hardening to an almost unrecognizable grimness.

"What are you going to do about this girl, now you've got her?"

"You leave her to me. I have plans for Miss Kelly Hartly."

Kelly shivered. An instant later, there was the macabre sound of cheerful resignation in the other man's tone as he replied, "You're the boss!"

"In that capacity, I suggest you get back over there before the senator gives you the slip."

"You'd think he would have sense enough to be scared."

"Brave men are sometimes foolish men," Charles answered.

"On second thought," the guard said, his tone wheedling, "How about trading jobs with me? I wouldn't mind watching the one you got cornered at all. Must be a lot more fun keeping a pretty girl under wraps than an old geezer."

There was distaste in Charles's voice as he replied,

"Thank you, no. You would be better to keep your mind on what you're doing."

"Don't get riled. It was just an idea. See you later."

At the sound of retreating footsteps, Kelly jerked to attention, moving as quickly as she could from her place beside the door. She circled toward the kitchen in clumsy haste. There, she held to the cabinet, taking several deep breaths, trying to still the trembling that seized her.

No matter what she had thought, or what she had told herself, she had not really believed the situation to be as bad as she had imagined. The hint that it was even more so, that death might be in store for the man they were holding, that Charles had definite plans of his own for her, left her numb and shaken. She was also very aware that a part of her sickness was caused by the fact that she had not wanted to believe it.

It was some minutes before Charles came into the kitchen. By that time, Kelly had regained some semblance of composure. She looked up from peeling slices of bacon apart and dropping them into the electric skillet to return his greeting with a cool good morning.

"You don't have to do that," he said.

"You didn't have to bring me coffee this morning either, but you did." It was odd how normal he looked, not at all as if he had been discussing the death of a human being.

"As a peace offering it seems to have been a failure."

"Next time, try leaving it outside the door." Where the courage came from to speak so boldly to him she did not know, but she could not bring herself to look at him while she spoke.

"You couldn't have reached it from there. Besides, wouldn't that have been a little ridiculous when the door was open already?"

"Not from choice."

"Is that what this is all about, offended modesty?"

51

"That's the least of it," she told him, "but if you want to start a list, you can put that on it somewhere."

He stood watching her a moment, his gaze on her slim fingers as she picked up a fork and began to line up the slices of bacon in the pan. Moving to the sink, he washed his hands, then found bread, butter, and a cookie sheet. As with a liberal hand he applied butter to the bread to be toasted under the broiler he said, "I am assuming it's the pain in your foot that's making you so waspish this morning."

"You assume wrong."

"Then it doesn't hurt? That's good."

It might be better to let him think that the injury was worse than it was. If he saw her having difficulty getting around, then he might be less watchful, less on his guard. "I didn't say that."

"I'll look at it after breakfast."

"That—won't be necessary."

"Kelly, my sweet," he said pausing, "are we going to have to go through all this again?"

"Not if you don't try to force me to do things I don't want. And I am not your sweet," she answered with a lift of her chin and a quick glance at him from the corner of her eye.

He ignored the last. "Even if it's for your own good? For the next few days, we are going to have to stay here together. If you will accept that, and stop fighting me, you can still rest and relax, enjoy your vacation."

"Relax? After what you have said to me, and done?"

The incredulity in her voice was not feigned. He frowned. "I could say you brought it on yourself, but I won't. I can promise that you will be completely safe if you will agree to a truce."

She sent him a look of scorn. "And I'm to take your word for that?"

"I assure you," he said softly, his grip tightening on

the knife he held until his knuckles gleamed white, "that you need nothing more."

Kelly felt her nerves tighten as she recognized the thread of danger in his tone. Once before she had dared to doubt his word. It seemed he did not take such slurs lightly. "For how long?"

"Until the end of the week."

"Couldn't you wind up whatever it is that you are doing before then, and let me have the last few days of my time off in peace?"

"I'm afraid not."

She should have known. Despite the firm sound of his voice just now, he had mentioned, when he was talking to the guard, the possibility of it being as much as two weeks before the pay off came. A frown between her eyes, she took up the bacon and set it to drain on the paper towel. Cracking eggs into the hot fat, she said, "There're still a few things I don't understand."

"Is it necessary that you should?"

"You would prefer that I take things on faith, as if you were God?"

He let his breath out slowly. "I'm sure it's too much to expect, but it would be convenient."

He stepped to slide the toast under the broiler. As he straightened, the light from the window over the sink slanted across the planes of his face with sharp clarity, highlighting the small split in the smooth line of his upper lip, and the long, raw-looking mark of a nail burn down his neck. The sight of the damage she had inflicted gave her no joy, though it did have the effect of making her lose track, temporarily, of what she had been saying.

She did not speak again until they were seated at the breakfast table. The savory smell of the bacon and hot buttered toast was usually enough to spark her appetite, but this morning all she could do was push the food around on her plate. Charles's appreciation of his breakfast was unimpaired. He ate the two eggs she had cooked him with every sign of enjoyment, then spread grape jelly on the remaining pieces of toast, topping them off with another cup of hot coffee.

She shot him a quick look from under her lashes. Choosing her words carefully, she said, "If you won't tell me who you are, can you at least tell me where you come from?"

"There's nothing mysterious about that," he said after a moment. "I'm from south Louisiana, just above New Orleans to be exact."

She had thought as much. "Your accent, then, is—"

"French Creole, which means—"

"I know. Of French descent born in a foreign country, foreign to France, that is."

"Good for you. Most people seem to think it has something to do with mixed heritage, mixed blood. Nothing could be further from the truth."

His praise was oddly satisfying. "I've never traveled much in south Louisiana, never met many true French-speaking people from that region, but I've read a great deal about it." Before the words had left her mouth, she recalled one important fact. New Orleans was the center for one of the best-organized, best-known Mafia families in the nation. A cold feeling moved over her, and she suppressed a shiver that left gooseflesh along her arms.

"I thought you said you were from this state," he said, his voice sharpening, "a friend of the judge's daughter?"

"I am, but I've never had the money to travel. As for Mary, she lives above here, in north Louisiana. There's a world of difference."

"You're right, of course," he said smoothly. "You are Scotch-Irish, I imagine, staunchly Baptist, and sternly disapproving of the hard-playing, hard-drinking, but deeply religious Catholics in my part of the state."

"Not at all. I wouldn't be so stupidly prejudiced."

"Then why do you look at me with so much dislike in your eyes?"

"I—surely I don't have to tell you that?"

He leaned back, his long brown fingers toying with his coffee cup. "If your feelings are for me personally, perhaps they can be changed."

"I doubt it," she told him, her voice flat.

"Is that a challenge?"

Her head came up and she stared at him. She did not like the way he was watching her, nor the lazy smile that lurked in the depths of his dark eyes. "Certainly not!"

"Too bad. I might have enjoyed making you reconsider."

"It would have been a waste of time."

"But what else is there to spend it on?"

She crumpled the paper towel she was using as a napkin and dropped it into her plate. Gathering her silverware and empty coffee cup, she set these on top of the napkin, pushing plate and all away from her. When she glanced up again, the gaze of the man across the table was still upon her. She looked out the window, then clasped her fingers together, staring down at them. When she lifted her lashes once more, his attention was fastened on her wrists, traveling slowly along her arms to her shoulders, brushing her mouth and small straight nose, finally clashing with the expression in her gray eyes.

"I wish," she said distinctly, "that you wouldn't do that."

"Do what?" he asked innocently.

"Watch me like that."

"Like what?"

She would give anything now if she had never spoken. "You know very well what I mean! As if you meant to make me self-conscious."

"Do I?"

"Why not," she cried, "since I don't know what you're thinking, what you mean to do next!"

He leaned forward, catching her hands in his warm grasp, speaking her name with a soft, musical inflection it had never had before. "Don't do this, don't tear yourself apart in this way. If you would just accept—"

He stopped abruptly, turning her wrists upward on the table, his gaze fastening on the purple bruises that marred the blue-veined fragility of her skin. Kelly tried to pull her hands away, but he would not allow it.

"Did I do that?" he asked, his voice low.

"Who else?" Kelly let her breath out slowly as she gave up the uneven struggle. "I suppose you are going to say that's something else I brought on myself?"

He shook his head. With his thumbs, he massaged her bruised flesh with a movement curiously gentle and soothing. "I'm sorry that it had to be this way."

"If you were really sorry, you would let me go," she said tentatively.

"I can't do that."

"Can't, or won't?" Her voice was bitter as she read the finality of his tone.

He released her, coming to his feet, kicking back his chair. The shadow of irony overlaying the grimness in his dark eyes, he said, "Both."

Kelly sat where she was for some time after he strode from the room, heading down the hall. She spread her hands flat on the wood-grain surface of the round oak table, pressing them down to still their shaking. Her thought processes were anything but concise. She went over the same ground again and again, trying to make sense of a smile, a word, a gesture. What was the purpose behind his offer of a truce? Had it been meant to lull her into a sense of security? He was a persuasive man, was Charles. It had not been easy holding out against his soft phrases and the look of concern in his eyes. But should she have held out, that was the question. What was there to be gained by keeping to her animosity? Her straight-forward defiance kept him on his guard, whereas, if she should abide by his truce, he might become so complacent that he would cease to keep such careful watch.

There was another possibility that had occurred to her. Why couldn't she make some use of this physical attraction he seemed to feel for her? If he thought she was falling victim to his charms, he might be even less likely to keep her under his eyes every minute of the day and night.

She would have to be careful. It would not do to capitulate too quickly. After her uncompromising stand, nothing would be more likely to arouse his suspicions. She would have to be subtle in her role as smitten female. He was not the kind of man to take lightly being used in such a way. More than that, if she should proceed too quickly and convincingly, she might well find herself with a more positive physical reaction from him than she was prepared to handle. It was not part of her plans to share his bed voluntarily, sacrificing self-respect and honor for the sake of her neck. If it should come to that, she would have the satisfaction of fighting him tooth and nail, of leaving him more to remember her by than a split lip and a nail burn down his neck.

Because she had nothing else to do, Kelly cleared away the dishes, returning the gold-and-brown kitchen to its former state of shining cleanliness. While she was at the sink, she heard Charles go out. A short time later, she heard the rumble of a motor as it was kicked into life. Moving out onto the veranda, she was in time to see a man in a boat leaving the clump of trees further along the shoreline, the sleek white craft making a wide arc as it headed out across the lake. It must have been the burly guard from the guest cottage, for Charles could be seen coming along the shore, making his way from the spot from which the boat had left.

The boathouse was just there, Kelly remembered.

The judge had built it nearer to the guest cottage than the main house since he did not want it blocking his view of the lake. But though the low-lying wooden structure protected an ancient aluminum fishing boat that she and the Kavanaugh brood had paddled everywhere, and also a fiberglass bass boat fitted up with high-powered outboard motor, trolling motor, depth finder, and every other gadget for ferreting out sport fish, the judge had never owned such a fast and expensive rig as was disappearing in the distance.

Where was the guard going in such a hurry? How long would he be away? And while he was gone who was going to guard the elderly man Charles had called "the senator"? Did Charles expect to be able to handle both him and herself, or was the older man lying bound and gagged, or perhaps drugged, alone in the guest cottage?

Kelly swung away from the door, a sick sensation in the pit of her stomach. She did not feel like facing Charles just now. With such thoughts preying on her mind, she was afraid she could not be civil to him, much less conciliatory.

In her room, Kelly busied herself making up the bed, straightening and putting things away. It was only as she had her suitcase half unpacked and its contents put away in the closet and dresser drawers that she realized how far she had come toward accepting the situation, rather than just pretending. She hesitated a moment, then decided with a shrug to finish the job. She might as well be thorough since she would not put it past Charles to inspect her room at any time.

She could not stop thinking about the senator. Though she combed her memory, she could not put a name to his face. He was definitely not one of the congressmen currently representing the state in Washington. The year before had been an election year, and the names and faces of the men who had achieved such high office had been plastered all over billboards, advertising posters, fliers, and calling cards, to say nothing of television. Nor did she think that the old gentleman was one of those defeated in the hard-fought campaign. The men elected to conduct business in the senate chambers at the state capital in Baton Rouge were just as well known. Politics had never been of much interest to her, but she felt that even she could recognize anyone as widely known as that.

Where did that leave her? Could he possibly be from out of state, a congressman from Texas or Mississippi, or even farther afield? She had no idea, but it seemed as good a guess as any.

But if it were true, what could the Louisiana Mafia possibly want with him? Was he a wealthy man, the head of a corporation? Was he, that genial, quiet-looking little man, the head of another Mafiosa family?

It was wild, incredible. The Mafia was something you read about in the paper, something that was spoken of in grim voices on the evening news. It had nothing to do with people like her, ordinary, everyday people. Kidnapping was a crime of terrorists, something that happened in Europe or South America, not in a quiet, backwater fishing camp in the heart of central Louisiana. She was wrong, she must be. And yet, what other explanation was there?

Her shoulder bag still lay on the bedside table. Picking it up, she carried it to the dresser where she began to unload her lip gloss and mascara, her sunscreen and tanning lotion and moisturing lotion, the few items she felt were necessary for a few days of simple living. With those things removed, placed in a neat line on the dresser, the bag felt oddly light.

Kelly opened the bag wide, then in disbelief, turned the contents out onto the surface of the dresser. Sunglasses, breath mints, a mirrored compact, a packet of tissue, a few receipts, a notepad and pencil, a small hairbrush, and a handful of coins clattered into a pile, but there was no sign of her billfold.

She had been robbed. With the exception of a few cents in change, all the money she had was gone, and all her identification taken.

Flinging down the empty bag, Kelly stormed from the room, limping down the hall. She found Charles in the kitchen, pouring himself a glass of ice water from the pitcher kept in the refrigerator. She came to a stop, slivers of ice glinting in her gray eyes and her breath coming quickly with her agitation.

"Where," she demanded, "is my money?"

He turned to look at her, one eyebrow lifted. Before he answered, he replaced the pitcher, shut the refrigerator door, drank his water, and put the glass in the sink. Turning back he said, "Are you accusing me of stealing?"

The steely displeasure in his voice did not deter her. "My money is gone, and you are the only other person in this house."

"Very true, but do you actually think I would want your money?"

His meaning penetrated the haze of anger that gripped her. Her lips compressed. "You may not have wanted or needed the little I had, but it's gone, and no one except you could have taken it."

"Now why would I do that?"

"I expect it was to keep me from using it to get away from here!"

"Then you concede that I may not be a thief. That's progress of a sort."

She distrusted his smile and the easy manner that he had assumed. "That may be, but it doesn't tell me what you did with my billfold."

"It doesn't, does it?" he agreed, unperturbed. "Don't be alarmed; you'll get it back—eventually."

Here it was, her first opportunity to carry through with her plan. She forced herself to meet his dark gaze. "I—I suppose it is, progress, I mean."

"Truce?" he queried softly, his head tilted to one side.

She lowered her lashes. "Truce."

"I think I'll hold you to it, even if the word did nearly choke you."

She flashed him a look of purest dislike.

"That's better," he murmured. "If you get too meek and quiet on me, I may have to start wondering if you are up to something."

"You make it sound as if you don't really want a truce at all," she said in frustrated resentment.

A smile moved over his face, lighting his eyes. "You may be right. Sparring with you hasn't been all bad."

"Or all one-sided," she answered with a meaningful nod from the bruises on her wrists to the scratch left by her nail on his neck and the cut on his lip.

He touched his mouth with one knuckle, a rueful look in his eyes. "You're right about that."

It was ridiculous, but his admission had the effect of soothing her ruffled dignity and sense of injury. "Now that is settled," she said, "what are we going to do?"

"That's up to you." His dark gaze was fastened on her with a narrow look of interest.

"If you have been here several days, you must have some idea of what the choices are."

He gave a thoughtful nod. "Swimming is out, at least until your foot heals a little more; incidentally, I'm still going to have a look at that."

"If you must," she said, schooling her voice to indifference.

He gave her a dark glance before he went on. "We could take a walk, but there again, you have a handicap."

"Not if it's a short walk."

"True," he agreed. "That might be arranged then."

"I'll get my shoes."

She allowed herself a sign of irritated impatience as she correctly interpreted the gaze he directed toward

61

her bare feet. Moving with a halting step to the dining table, she held to it with one hand while she lifted her foot and peeled aside the tape. She refused to look at him as he approached. It was a complete surprise when his hands closed about her waist, and she was lifted to sit upon the table.

Her hands came up automatically to rest on his arms as she steadied herself. For a long instant, their eyes met, then he released her and stepped back. Bending, he inspected his handiwork.

His nearness, the impersonal touch of his hands, affected Kelly with a feeling of unwilling agitation. Sternly she resisted the wayward impulse to touch the dark, crisp waves of his hair. It was strictly a physical reaction to his strength and the power he exercised over her at this moment in time; she knew that. There had been a great deal written in the last few years of the strange relationships that could spring up between captor and captive. Still, it was frightening, not the least reason being that it made it necessary for her to be wary of herself, and her own emotions.

When she had fetched her sandals and slipped into them, they left the house. They turned in the direction of the open stretch of the lake by mutual accord, Charles matching his pace to her progress.

As the morning advanced, it was growing hotter; it was already past the stage that could be called warm. The dew had already evaporated from the grass, and where the long, uncut lawn had been crushed underfoot, the warm sun brought out a smell like the scent of a hay meadow. Their footsteps flushed crickets and grasshoppers from their path that scattered with tiny, clicking noises in the silence. Everything was still; not a leaf or a strand of gray moss moved. The lake glittered with a dazzling brilliance, reflecting the blue of the sky overhead in its brown-green waters. At its verge was a crisp green edging of tender marsh plants covered with tiny white blooms. In the sun-struck shallows, clear enough to see the sand on the bottom, minnows darted. A black water bug skated away over the surface. In the shadows of the nearby cypress trees was the mossy snag of a downed tree trunk, barely rising above the water. Upon it sat a row of turtles that slipped off one by one with gentle plopping sounds as Charles and Kelly drew near. Their approach also disturbed a white crane from its perch in the top of a dead tree, and it lifted off with a great flapping of wings. From somewhere close, hidden among the leaves of a moss-hung white oak, came the monotonous croaking of a tree frog, a sound the judge had always insisted told of coming rain.

Kelly knelt at the water's edge. From the debris washed up by the waves—the dried grass, strings of blackened water-weeds, and bits of rotted leaves and wood—she plucked a cypress ball, straightening with it in her hand. Small, not much larger than a marble, colored a pale celadon green, it had the look of carved jade.

To break the silence between her companion and herself Kelly said, "Mary and I used to string these things for necklaces."

"Mary Kavanaugh?"

She bit back a sharp retort, settling instead for a nod. "We had a lot of fun in those days, Mary, Peter, Mark, and I. The boys built a diving platform out there in the trees, beyond the swimming raft in the deeper water on the other side of the catwalk. You had to be careful how you jumped off it, though, because of the stumps underwater. The first time Peter dived, he had to have seven stitches in the top of his head. I was so scared I was nearly sick when he came up covered with blood, mainly because I had a crush on him at the time."

"One of the judges's sons?" he said, a rough note in his voice.

63

"I thought you knew the judge," she said, unable to keep the suspicion from her tone.

"I never said so. I only said he lent me the house."

"Isn't that a little odd?"

His face was expressionless as he said, "We—have mutual friends."

What possible connection could there between Judge Kavanaugh and this man? By no stretch of the imagination could Kelly conceive of so fine and upstanding a man as the judge having anything to do with criminals or the families that made up the Mafia. It was an angle she had not stopped to consider before. Perhaps the explanation was that the mutual friend was the man they called the senator. Could he have accepted the loan of the lake house only to find himself a prisoner there? How conveniently that would have worked out for Charles and his friend the guard.

Unconsciously, Kelly turned to look at the guest cottage. There was a better view of it from here than from the main house. The same was true of the wood-and-metal boathouse in its covering of trees off to their left. "I saw the other man leave a little while ago in the speedboat," she said, her tone casual. "I suppose that's the way you and the others came to the house?"

"A brilliant deduction," he told her, his manner openly mocking.

"I don't see the point, not if you are posing as residents."

"Boats leave no tracks, and are harder to trace than automobiles."

"I thought they had to be registered."

"Oh, yes, and marked with a registration number—put on with nice stick-on lettering that is easily changed."

Kelly glanced at the guest house again, "It's none of my business, but didn't the departure of your accomplice leave you in something of a bind?"

"In what way?"

"There's only one of you to watch two of us." Her attention was caught by the faint sound of a radio coming from the cottage, or was it a television? There was an antenna at the back, poking up among the trees.

"Your concern for your fellow prisoner is touching. Are you afraid he will get away and you won't?"

She turned a cold look on him. "Hardly. If there was any danger of that, you wouldn't be so nonchalant about it. What troubles me is what you may have done to him to give you such peace of mind."

He did not move, did not speak, and yet she sensed the force of the anger that surged through him. He reached out to cup her elbow, and it was as though an electric current had touched her. His voice soft, he said, "Would you believe me if I told you he was up there being mesmerized by game shows and soap operas he never had the chance to watch before?"

"What keeps him from just—leaving?"

"He has no car, the boathouse is locked, his heart isn't good—no walking you see? Besides, it may be he likes the utter relaxation of letting someone else do the thinking, make the decisions, while he is saved from the need to see and be seen."

"No," she said, "I don't believe it."

"Shall we go and visit with him then?" His fingers tightened on her arm.

It was then that they heard the motorboat. They swung back at the sound, watching the speeding white launch come toward them like a silver streak, its wake spreading out in a wide fan as the boat made a great curve, circling to come into the landing beside the catwalk.

"I would have thought that to be inconspicuous was what you wanted," Kelly murmured. "If so, I can't say much for your choice of transportation."

"Sometimes other considerations are more important," he answered, but there was a brooding quality in his tone. He was still frowning when the other man stepped off the near end of catwalk and came toward them.

The guard had removed his gun, donned a gold nylon life vest and placed an open mesh cap squarely on his head. Regardless, he looked nothing like a fisherman. Kelly's eyes widened as she recognized what he held in his hand.

"Everything checks out," the guard said, holding out her denim-covered billfold to Charles. "I placed the transatlantic call, but couldn't reach the party you wanted, some mix-up in the itinerary. I left a message. You should get a cable tonight or tomorrow with the information you wanted, the time difference being what it is."

Charles's narrowed gaze met that of the other man in obvious understanding. "No problems?"

"No problems."

"Did you get the sen——our other guest's ice cream?"

The other man snapped his fingers. "Left it in the boat. I'd better get it before it melts."

Charles turned back toward the path that led to the main house, his grip still fastened on Kelly's arm. She did not move, holding back. "I thought we were going to see about the——the old man?"

"There's no need now. He has company again."

"Company? That's isn't exactly what I would call it."

"I'm sure, but what's in a name?"

Kelly paid no attention to his wry question. "You don't intend to take me, do you?"

"I've changed my mind," he answered, amusement rising in his eyes as he took in her pugnacious attitude.

"Why?"

"I told you once that you have an expressive face. It appears your imagination pictures all kinds of horrors being visited upon a helpless old gentleman. So long as you are uncertain whether you are right, you may think twice before you step out of line."

Rage flared over her, followed by sudden chill of fear. Under such stimulous, her mind was prodded into action. "On the other hand," she said quietly, "I might be forced to conclude that if I had seen him I would no longer have anything to fear."

"So you might," he agreed, a gleam in his eyes that might have been admiration, but could also have been expectation.

It was diabolical. She could take what he was doing to mean either that she was perfectly safe or that she stood in the deadliest danger. The only thing that could give her any hint of which to count on was her own conception of the kind of man she was facing.

"You abominable, impossible, conniving—"

"Careful," he warned, tilting his head on one side. "We have a truce, but if you are the one to break it, I refuse to be responsible for what I might do!"

✤ Chapter 5 ✤

Her best defense, Kelly decided, was to pretend
there was nothing unusual going on, to proceed as
though she were alone. Toward that end, she an-
nounced her intention of spending the rest of the morning sunbathing. Charles applauded the idea, falling in
with it immediately and with every sign of good humor.
He spread a piece of canvas on the grass where the
lawn sloped to the lake, the only place other than the
swimming raft where there was enough sun away from
the traveling shade of the trees.

Dressed in her swimsuit, armed with sunglasses, sunscreen, tanning lotion, her book, and her beach towel,
Kelly settled on the canvas. Charles, in the brief white
suit she remembered vividly from the day before, positioned himself beside her. They lay unmoving, without
speaking, soaking in the molten sunlight.

Within minutes, they were gilded with a fine sheen
of perspiration. It gathered in rivulets, running into
Kelly's hair, dampening the tresses at the nape of her
neck, gathering between her breasts.

"Your sunscreen and suntan lotion aren't going to
do you much good in the bottle," Charles said.

Drugged with heat, it was a moment before Kelly

could bring herself to form an answer. "I probably don't need it."

"You'll be as pink as a parboiled shrimp."

"I promise I won't ask you to take me to the hospital."

She heard the rustle of the canvas as he sat up, but she lay still. She had almost decided he had let the subject drop when she felt his hands on her face, smoothing across the bridge of her nose and the high bones of her cheeks.

Her eyes flew open. She met his dark, smiling gaze as he leaned over her. Before she could speak, he said, "Sunscreen."

She could attend to the protection of her skin as he thought she should, or she could lie where she was and accept his ministrations. It was the treacherous urge to do the latter that made her sit up and snatch the tube of sunscreen from his hand.

Satisfied, he lay back down, locking his hands behind his head as he watched her. His appreciative gaze traveled over her curves, accented by a modestly revealing, aqua-blue bikini. When she substituted the tanning lotion for the sunscreen, he followed her movements as she rubbed it over her arms and shoulders and along the length of her torso and legs.

"Would you like me to do your back?" he asked, his tone dulcet.

"Thank you, no, I can manage," she answered, the glance she sent him edged with distrust. She did, too, though not without difficulty. Her chore completed, Kelly lay back down. The scent of her lotion hung in the still and humid air.

"You smell like coconut candy," he drawled, "good enough to eat."

The timbre of his voice seemed to vibrate through her. Keeping her voice casual with an effort, she said, "You are welcome to use some of my lotion, if you like."

"I probably don't need it," he answered, a silky note to his voice.

It crossed her mind to treat him as he had treated her, by applying a sample of the sunscreen. She was by no means sure that he would object, as she had, to being anointed with lotion and coconut oil, however. He might even enjoy it. In any case, as brown as his skin was, he was doubtless right; he would have little use for it.

The quiet between them lengthened, disturbed only by the persistent croaking of the tree frog. The sun bore down upon them, bringing a flush of heat to their skin, running like fever in their blood. And then from the man beside her came one soft-spoken word. "Chicken."

There was something in what he said, she had to admit, though she gave no sign that she had heard. She was more than a little hesitant to begin her program of appearing to be smitten by his charm. She was also reluctant to risk his reaction to a question that exercised her mind. It was annoying to be forced to concede that he had the power to affect her with such trepidation. It must be resisted.

"Tell me, just what was that man doing with my billfold? What did he mean, that everything 'checked out'?"

"Can't you guess?" His voice was lazy, unconcerned.

She turned her head to look at him as he lay with his eyes closed beside her. "You had him verify that I am who I said?"

"And that you do indeed work for your construction firm, and have no record, not even so much as a parking violation."

"How could you find out all that in such a short time?"

"Computers are wonderful things."

"You have to have the authority to use them, first."

"It does pay to have friends in high places," he agreed, his firm mouth curving in the faintest of smiles.

She was no closer to knowing what to make of him than she had ever been. It was plain, however, that he had no intention of enlightening her beyond what he wanted her to know, or what was self-evident. Setting her teeth in exasperation, she closed her eyes and tried once more to relax.

They consumed a light lunch of chef's salad, crackers, and a tall, cooling drink. Afterward, Kelly showered and shampooed her hair. Before she left the bathroom, she pulled on her shorts and top once more, then with resignation, rebandaged her foot. If she didn't see to it, Charles doubtless would. Before the dresser in the bedroom, she combed the tangles from her hair, then left it to dry naturally, only raking her fingers through it now and then to speed the process. She felt headachy and on edge. Though the air conditioning had been switched on once more and it was cool in the room, there was an oppressive feeling in the air.

She wondered where Charles was, and what he was doing. Though she could not hear him moving about, she was almost certain he was somewhere nearby. It didn't matter, of course. She would be glad of a few hours' respite from his constant presence, if he would allow it.

She threw herself down on the bed and picked up her book. By furious concentration, she was able to become involved in the story after a time. Slowly, as the effect of the sun and the warm water of her shower wore away, she began to grow cool. The air conditioning was certainly more than effective, for beyond the drapes at the window, the wearing heat of the afternoon could be sensed.

Rising from the bed, she turned the bedspread down, then lay back down, slipping her feet and lower legs beneath it. She picked up her book again, but her

71

eyes felt grainy and raw from her sleepless night and the sun's glare this morning. She turned her book face down and let her lids fall, pressing them tightly closed.

A booming sound echoed over the house. Kelly opened her eyes. The light in the room was dim, bordering on darkness, and the air stale. From her stiffness, and the heaviness that clung to her mind, she thought she had been asleep for some time.

Once more the thudding boom rolled over the roof above her. Thunder. It was going to rain; the judge and the tree frog had been right. Her whimsical smile was banished by a sudden yawn. Despite the time she had been asleep, she did not feel rested or refreshed in any way. Shaking her head, she sat up and slid from the bed. She threw the spread up over the pillows and tucked it under them, then smoothed out the wrinkles. Pausing in the task, she stood listening, thinking she heard the rain already, but it was only the rustling of the leaves of the live oaks overhead in the rising wind.

Drawn by the sound of the storm, she left her room. She moved through the house, letting herself out onto the veranda. There were rocking chairs and heavy wooden lounges ranged along the inside wall, but she skirted them, heading for a porch swing on the far end. Dropping into it, she positioned herself in the corner and swung her feet up onto the seat. From that end of the house, nearer the cottage, she could see out over the open lake, could watch the storm that was brewing.

Her attention was riveted suddenly by a movement in the water. It was Charles on the swimming raft. Had he seen her there in the shadowy dimness of the screened porch? More likely, he had heard the closing of the front door as she came outside and realized she was awake. Whatever the reason, he came smoothly to his feet and dived, cutting the water with scarcely a splash. The waters of the lake seemed to catch and hold what little light was left in the evening sky, for she could see the dark outline of his head and shoulders as he cleaved the water with smooth, strong strokes.

He reached the catwalk and pulled himself up the ladder nailed to its side near the boat landing. The white speedboat was no longer there; it must have been hidden away once more in the boathouse.

As Charles started along the catwalk, silver lightning flickered in the sky, striking down into the open water behind him. For an instant, the dark outline of his figure was illuminated in eerie light. It gave him the look of a statue cast in ancient, gleaming bronze come to life, with the gold disk at his neck glittering like a baleful beacon.

Pain, and a strange species of fear half for him, half for herself, moved in Kelly's chest. The thunder that followed the lightning reverberated along her nerves. There was something in the elemental forces gathering around her that made her feel vulnerable, and at the same time sent the quicksilver rise of excitement like champagne to her head. Watching Charles as he drew closer, she clasped her hands around her drawn-up knees, closing her fingers tightly together to still their trembling. She was going to have to be careful. How much longer she could live on the knife-edge of her emotions without doing something desperately foolhardy, she did not know. That balancing act was the reason she was so affected by the mere sight of the man who was holding her captive; it must be.

Charles paused just inside the screen door of the veranda. His face was a blur in the dimness, but she thought he was staring in her direction.

"It's going to rain," she said, and was immediately aware of the inanity of the comment, though powerless to do anything about it.

"So it seems." His agreement was cool.

"Didn't anyone ever tell you to stay out of the water when it's lightning?"

"Were you worried?"

"About you, no. But it did cross my mind that I might be better off with you alive." Her tone was as casual as she could manage.

"How is that?" There was a taut sound in his voice.

"As they say, 'Better the devil you know—' "

"I might have guessed," he said, and moved with swift strides into the house.

Kelly swallowed against the tightness in her throat, at the same time, narrowing her eyes against the wind that swept across the veranda. The great branches of the live oaks overhead creaked and groaned. The clatter of their leaves was loud in the stillness. From near the lake there came a chorus of tree frogs, mocked by the deep honking of the huge bull frogs. Far out on the lake could be seen the white frosting of foam as the surface of the water was blown into waves. The porch swing began to move, pushed by the blown gusts that struck the house. As thunder rumbled again, the smell of ozone, sharp and fresh, filled the air. The heat of the day was banished, to be replaced by a cool and tingling freshness.

Lightning crackled again, illuminating the veranda with its blue-white flare. Kelly flinched and got to her feet, ready to retreat into the house, yet reluctant to leave the fiery display. At the guest cottage, lights bloomed in the increasing blackness of the evening, a yellow glow half obscured by the waving branches of the trees. The chains of the porch swing began to creak as it swung back and forth. Leaves and the torn ends of branches whirled through the air to be plastered against the wire screen that hummed in the wind.

A footstep sounded behind her, and Charles moved to stand at her side. He had changed into pants and an open-necked sports shirt. There was about him a warm, male smell overlaid by the spiciness of the soap that he used in his shower. As if a signal had been received, the rain came roaring toward them over the lake, churning the water to froth, spattering through

74

the trees, drumming the ground to bring forth the smell of warm wet earth. It pounded on the roof, and struck against the screen in a mighty rush that sent mist fogging in the air, swirling toward them. They backed away to the house wall. In the deafening, wind-swept fury of the storm, it was a moment before Kelly realized that she was shivering with the damp chill, or that Charles had put his arm around her, holding her against him. As if drawn by something beyond her control, Kelly lifted her lashes to look at him. He was watching her in the semidarkness, his face without expression. Slowly, by almost imperceptible degrees, giving her ample time to draw back, he lowered his head and touched his mouth to hers. His lips were warm and firm, and her own molded to them in sweet accord.

What else could she do? She wanted him to think she was resigned, didn't she? She wanted him to believe that she was falling for him, if ever so little. Wasn't that the plan? Such thoughts were no more than brief flashes across the outermost surface of her mind as she melted against him, spreading her fingers over the muscled firmness of his chest.

He ended the kiss with a soft laugh. His voice low near her ear, he said, "That was very nice, *chérie*. I have been wondering what it would be like to have a little cooperation since the first time I held you."

Abruptly she pushed away from him. "So now you know."

"Yes," he said, an odd inflection in his voice, as if he were trying not to laugh, or else deliberately refraining from showing his annoyance. "And now, what would you like for dinner?"

The wind was diminishing, the thunder rumbling away. The rain had turned to a steady downpour that already showed signs of slackening to a soft, all-night drizzle.

Kelly moved a few steps further away from him. "Fish," she said over her shoulder. "I would like fresh-caught fish dipped in cornmeal and fried in hot fat."

"Sorry. Fish isn't on the menu."

"We always used to have it the second night we were here, after the judge and the boys had gone fishing." She went on, more for something to say than anything else. "Fresh fish, thick-sliced French fries, light, golden brown hush puppies with onion and pepper inside, and cole slaw."

"By the boys, you mean the judge's sons, I suppose. Which one was it you had the crush on?"

"Peter," she answered without looking at him.

"Do you still see him?"

It almost sounded as if he were jealous. "I haven't seen him in three years, not since I went off to secretarial college on my own."

"But you still care?" he inquired, his voice tight.

"Heavens, no. That was over years ago, after that one summer. Peter killed it quite dead himself when he put a handful of cold, dirty, wiggling fishing worms in my bed."

Positive amusement lacing his tone, he said, "That really was unforgivable."

"It was. Though the boys thought it was hilariously funny. The judge sentenced them to wash the sheets, but even he thought it was comical. Girls that age have such a strong sense of outraged disgust."

"I would have liked to have seen you at that age."

"I doubt you would have been impressed," she said, giving her head a reminiscent shake. "I was all hair, eyes, legs, and injured feelings."

"A charming picture." His comment was quiet.

"Yes, isn't it?" she said wryly, and turned quite naturally to smile at him. "I don't know how the judge and his wife put up with me."

"Easily, I should think," he answered, a soft note she had not heard before in his voice.

Why did he have such power to disconcert her? She

was continually off balance in his presence, never certain of her ground. She could almost believe it was deliberate, a campaign to confuse her, to prevent her thought processes from becoming too coherent so she might figure out exactly what he was doing. If that were the case, it was working admirably.

As he reached out to touch her arm, she drew in her breath with a sharp sound. "May I remind you that we had an agreement. You gave me your promise that I would be free from molestation."

He drew back as if he had been slapped. It was a moment before he answered, but when he did, the words held no heat. "You are entirely correct, and from now on I will do my best to remember."

"Good," she said, though the triumph she would have expected from his concession was missing.

"About dinner. I'm afraid the best I can offer is ham and eggs, unless you would like to do the honors."

The ham and eggs became omelets filled with chopped ham and flavored with shallots and a sprinkling of herbs. With it they ate a crusty loaf of French bread. Charles drank white wine with his repast, while Kelly, who was not used to wine with her meals, settled for water. Afterward, when the dishes had been cleared, she accepted a glass of Alsatian Riesling. With Charles carrying the bottle by its neck, they moved into the living room. He set his glass and the wine to one side, drew out a small phonograph from the bookcase cabinet, and set up a stack of records to play. The selections were classical, the first being a Chopin sonata, one of Kelly's favorites. Unless the tastes of the judge and Mrs. Kavanaugh had changed, the records must belong to Charles. The judge tended to prefer country and western music above all others, while his wife was happiest with string instrumentals and Broadway show tunes.

The rain dripped from the eaves, making gurgling, splashing sounds that seemed to blend with the music.

77

The air conditioning had been turned off and the doors thrown open to the rainy night. The leather couch, as Kelly settled herself in one corner, had a damp feel to it because of the humidity. Charles moved to stand in the doorway, staring out into the drenched darkness beyond the veranda. Kelly let her glance touch his broad back for an instant, then shifted her gaze to the bookcases with their collection of westerns, murder mysteries, historical romances, and back issues of *National Geographic*. She thought of going to her bedroom for her book, then decided against it. As long as Charles showed no sign of settling down to some such innocuous way of passing the evening, she could not either.

"Do you play gin rummy?" he asked, turning to lean in the door frame.

"Not very well."

"Scrabble? I believe there's a board in the cabinet."

She gave him a level look. "You don't have to entertain me."

"I was thinking of myself."

"Were you?" she inquired skeptically. "You don't seem like the gin-rummy type to me."

"And just how do I strike you?"

She tilted her head. "Book, pipe, and slippers?"

"Close," he agreed, one corner of his mouth tugging in a smile, "though I don't smoke."

"Or else a good restaurant, the theater, and a few night clubs before dawn."

"Closer still, but don't stop there."

"Playboy Club?"

"Wrong," he answered with a grimace. "I prefer my women without rabbit ears, false cleavage, and cuteness."

"Let me see, then," she said, narrowing her eyes. "Preservation Hall Dixieland jazz? *Café au lait* and *beignets* at the Cafe du Monde at three o'clock in the morning?"

"Are you certain you have never been to New Orleans?"

"I told you, I read a lot."

"You must let me take you there sometime."

"It seems unlikely," she said, her tone sharp with the sudden desolation the rebuke cost her.

"Who can say?"

The hostage mentality worked both ways, she reminded herself. The captor enjoying complete control over another human being often experienced feelings of affection not unlike that of a parent for a child, especially if some form of communication could be established, and if the captive responded with the proper subservience. Charles felt responsible for her, perhaps even pitied her helplessness even though he himself was the cause.

She ran the tip of her tongue over her dry lips. She seemed to have lost the thread of what they were saying. Oh, yes, an occupation for Charles for the evening hours. "I—I suppose before I came the others kept you company, even stayed here with you?"

"Not really. I'm not addicted to television, and I prefer my privacy."

"Having me here must be a trial for you."

"Yes," he agreed, the smile creeping back into his eyes, "but not in the way that you mean."

Kelly did not dare to let herself think about that. "If you have something to read, I don't mind."

"I'm not certain," he said slowly, "that it wouldn't be more interesting exploring a few more of your opinions. For instance, what do you think of politics?"

She sent him a swift look, reminded of her earlier curiosity concerning him and the senator. "Not much. It seems to be a thankless undertaking for men of principles, or else a dirty game for men who have money, or want it."

"You don't like money," he queried softly.

"Of course I do," she answered with a quick gesture

79

of her wine glass, "but there are limits to what I will do for it."

"And men with money?"

"You don't seriously want an answer to that?" she asked, a frown between her eyes as she wondered what he was getting at.

"Why not? Or have you never considered the matter?"

"You would never believe that, would you? Men with money," she went on thoughtfully, then said with a sly look, "Old men or young men? Well, it doesn't matter. I don't like ostentation; flashy diamond rings, satin dinner jackets, or foot-long cigars. I don't like noisy sports cars that are expensive enough to be quieter. I don't like expensive houses built in the United States to look like something found in Europe. I don't like people who complain about the burden of sudden riches, nor old monied families who consider the wealth sufficient reason for their existence,"

When she came to a pause, he inserted skillfully, "Is there anything you do like?"

"Quiet elegance, old houses carefully restored, vintage automobiles, handsome old silver, hand-made lace—"

"I was speaking of the combination of money and men," he reminded her.

"That's harder," she said, tipping her head to one side, "since I haven't run across the two together very often. I suppose I like the experience that a certain amount of money gives a man; the knowledge of how to order in a restaurant, and how much to tip. I like the assurance and the dynamic sense of power you feel around the movers and shakers of the world."

"Fascinating," he commented.

She sipped at the golden liquid that filled the glass in her hand. "You needn't jeer. You asked what I thought, and I told you, but it doesn't mean anything. What a man is like has little to do with money."

"Most people have a hard time separating the two."

"By that I suppose you mean most women?"

"Unfortunately, yes, and before you pounce on that and accuse me of being a chauvinist, I think I will find that book!"

It had been a peculiar conversation. Lying in her bed some time later, listening to the softly falling rain, Kelly went over it in her mind. What had been his object in drawing out her opinions on the subject of politics, men, and money? What could they have to do with him, or with the situation they were in?

Could it be that there was a political motivation behind his kidnapping of the senator? Was he a radical of some sort, an activist fighting for the common man with nothing but contempt for politicians and wealthy men? If that were the case, then what did he think of the views she had expressed? Had she shown herself to be too much the moderate capitalist? Would he, as time went by, try to persuade her to his views?

She lay frowning up into the darkness above her, trying to sort out her own feelings. She held no brief for political terrorists, men who committed horrible deeds in the name of the common good; and yet, wasn't it better to think that what he was doing sprang from deep conviction instead of simple larceny?

What was she doing? Surely she was not attempting to condone what he had done? What was the matter with her that she could not hold her anger or resolution where he was concerned? He had only to smile at her, or look at her with that warm expression of humor in his eyes, and she began to make excuses for him. This must stop. No matter the reason, what he was doing was outside the law, an interference with the basic freedom of not one but two people, a crime for which the punishment would be life imprisonment. He had spoken with the utmost casualness of the death of the man he was holding and as far as she knew, he would be just as casual about her own demise.

Kelly arose early after a restless night. The effects were plain to see as she looked in the mirror while she ran a brush through her hair. She was pale, and beneath her eyes lay the blue shadows of fatigue. It didn't matter. She cared not at all what she looked like, and it certainly made no difference how she appeared to Charles. In fact, it might be all to the good if she presented herself looking wan and hollow-eyed, though she suspected that if he noticed at all, he would be more likely to send her back to bed with a sleeping pill than to be sympathetic.

A sleeping pill. Why hadn't she thought of it before? He had some with him, she thought. He had mentioned it when he was trying to force her to take his aspirins. If only he could be persuaded to down a few. While he was comatose, she could search his room, or even him personally, for her car keys and billfold. By the time he awoke, she could be miles away, telling her incredible tale to the police. It seemed that was the only way she was going to escape. He was much too light a sleeper, much too alert to her every movement, for anything else to be possible. She had only to wait until he left her alone in the house again, giving her the opportunity to search for the pills. Then she would have to manufacture an opportunity to slip them into his food or drink, that was all.

That was all? The mere thought of carrying out such a plan tied her stomach in knots. What he would do if he caught her at any stage was something she dared not contemplate. Still, she could not just do nothing, letting the minutes, hours, and days go by, accepting whatever he might say or do while she staked her future on a vague feeling that he was attracted to her. Such a thing would mean less than nothing, especially if she should prove a danger to him.

The rain had stopped in the early-morning hours. The sun was out, brightening the house with the peculiar golden light of September. Charles was seated at the table with a cup of coffee in front of him when she entered the dining area. He saluted her with the cup. "It's freshly made and still hot," he said. "I would have brought it to you, but that didn't go over too well yesterday morning."

She moved past him into the kitchen where she poured herself a cup of the steaming brew, then returned to slide into a chair at the round oak table.

"You are walking better this morning," he commented.

She had forgotten to limp. Her reply was short. "Yes."

His gaze flicked over her, returning to her face. "How would you like to go fishing?"

"Fishing?" Her head came up and she stared at him.

"It's the only way I know of to provide the fish dinner you were talking about."

"This morning?" she asked, enthusiasm slowly lighting the gray of her eyes.

"I don't see why not."

Her face fell. "We haven't anything to use for bait."

"I doubt the bream will be biting after the storm last night, but the striped bass are schooling, and the judge had a good assortment of rods and reels and artificial baits. Since he said we were free to make use of them, I intend to take him at his word. We may be lucky enough to catch a few bass to eat, and if not, it's still something to do."

So he was not immune to boredom, or the problem of spending long stretches of time with one person. "I suppose so," she agreed.

"I'm not particularly hungry just now. What about you?" As she shook her head, he went on. "We can pack something to eat in the middle of the morning then. We won't have to be in any hurry to return."

They weren't long in putting such a simple plan into action. Laying out a battered, much-used picnic basket, they loaded it with a box of raisins, a jar of dry roasted nuts, a can of processed meat, a loaf of bread, and a jar of pickles. While Charles was putting cold drinks on ice, Kelly ran to her room to slip on her blue bikini under her shorts and shirt. If the day grew as hot as she suspected it might, this would be a fine opportunity to work on her tan again. Also, you never could tell. It seemed unlikely there would be a chance to part company with Charles, considering how good a swimmer he was and what close quarters they would have to share in the boat, but it was best to be prepared.

It crossed her mind to dart into his room for a quick search of the medicine chest in his bathroom while he was busy in the kitchen. It was a good thing she did not act on the impulse, for as she emerged from her room, he was just leaving his also, after changing his pants and sports shirt for a pair of cut-off jeans and a tee-shirt.

A life vest had to be found for both of them, as well as a hat to protect their heads and faces from the sun, a suitable rod and reel each, and a tackle box containing a fair collection of lures, plastic worms, top-water baits, and all the other paraphernalia necessary for bringing home the catch. With these things in hand, they made their way to the boathouse. Charles unlocked it, and they stowed their gear in the judge's bass boat. There was another delay while the outboard motor, unused for some time, was checked out. Charles filled the double gas tanks from the drum of spare fuel, handed Kelly into the boat, and cranked the motor.

At last they were edging out into the lake, pushing an iridescent swell before the heavy boat, stirring a not unpleasantly fishy smell from the water. Their progress scared up a young family of ducks, half-grown birds that erupted from the water with a great squawking and flapping and tip-toeing over the surface before they took to flight. Kelly sat in the forward captain's chair of the two that were bolted to the bass boat, since the controls for the outboard motor were in the rear. She turned to Charles with a grin, her eyes alight with pleasure.

There was an invigorating purity to the air this morning, as though it had been washed clean by the rain. The sun was warm, and would be warmer still as the day wore on, but it lacked the sullen, oppressive strength of the day before. As the boat gathered speed, the wind in her face was agreeably fresh and sweet. Kelly sat at ease in the armchair while they wove in and out among the green fringed cypresses and the standing snags of trees long dead on their way to the channel of the lake. It was odd, but she trusted the instinct and ability of the man guiding the boat, even if she trusted him in nothing else.

✿ Chapter 6 ✿

Green Lake, like most in Louisiana, was a man-made lake. It had been constructed through the simple process of building a dam and spillway across a natural stream. The catch basin thus formed filled quickly, inundating thousands of acres, most of it woodland. Since the cost of clear-cutting the proposed lake site of trees was much too steep, the bulldozers were brought in beforehand to push out a main channel, usually along the deeper section of the old water course, and perhaps one or two minor channels. The timber left standing was gradually covered as the water rose. The pines and hardwoods died quickly; their bases rotted, and they fell, sinking beneath the waves where the process of disintegration continued. This along with constant dripping of sap from the living trees both in the lake and along the shore gave the water its customary dark and murky color. But the cypresses were trees of the swamplands; they thrived in watery conditions. And if one of them died, its wood was practically indestructible. After the passage of years, the cypress trees stood like sentinels guarding the lake channels, providing perches for egrets, cranes, herons, and water turkeys, while the mass of rotting timber beneath the surface made an excellent spawning ground for fish where the hatchlings could stay hidden for survival.

The judge had enjoyed pointing out such processes and their ecological balances and benefits. Humans, he said, when they dammed streams and rivers, were doing no more than another of Mother Nature's creatures, the beaver, would have done if he had gotten there first. In the meantime, a man with a little luck and a good fishing rig could catch himself a mess of mighty good eating.

There was no pretense to the judge, none at all. He had been a farm boy before he became a lawyer, then a judge. He was open and honest, with a healthy appreciation for his country heritage. That was another reason why it was so difficult to connect him in any way with Charles and his kidnapping of the senator. Frowning a little, Kelly shook her head.

They gathered still more speed as they reached the open channel. Charles seemed to know exactly where he was going. He did not hesitate, but here, away from the danger of underwater obstructions, opened the throttle and sent the boat flying. After a few minutes, he swerved into the side channel and cut the motor to a low rumble, decreasing their speed so as not to disturb the water, or the fish, in the clearing ahead of them. A sunlit area not much larger than a fair-sized house and ringed about with trees, Kelly recognized it at once as one of the judge's favorite bass holes.

Charles turned off the motor, and they drifted silently into the opening. When the boat was where he wanted it, he let down the lead anchor in the stern. He took out the rod and reel brought for her and attached a small silver-colored artificial fish while she waited impatiently.

"Do you know how to use one of these things?" he asked as he handed the fishing rig to her.

"I think so." Kelly had to bite the side of her jaw to

keep from smiling. There had been several times when she had outfished Peter, Mark, and the judge together.

He gave her a few brief instructions, then pointed out a likely-looking spot at the edge of the trees across the width of the clear space of water. Kelly measured the distance with her eye, drew back her rod, and with a snap of her wrist sent the bait singing toward the exact spot he had shown her.

"How was that?" she asked, her tone demurely innocent.

"Fine," he answered, though the glance he directed at her was dark with suspicion before he bent over his own rig.

They fished diligently. After a half-hour or so in one spot, Charles pulled up the anchor and Kelly let down the small, battery-operated trolling motor that was bolted to the front of the boat. It had a foot control so that ideally it could be operated from the back chair, but it had not worked right since the time Peter had caught his foot in the cable. Kelly had to switch it on from the front seat and use the projecting handle to guide the boat quietly to another vantage point.

By twelve o'clock the arms of the captain's chairs and every exposed surface of the boat were hot to the touch. The calendar might say that fall was less than two weeks away, but there on the lake it was still deep summer. None of the birds that flitted back and forth among the trees—the sparrows, woodpeckers, blue jays, and cardinals—had thought of heading south; most, in fact, would winter there. Every leaf on the trees was still as green as when it had reached maturity in June. The sun sparkled on the water, a breeze stirred through the trees, and Kelly could hear the humming of bees on a floating mat of water plants.

"It's a beautiful day," Kelly said suddenly.

Charles glanced at her, his lips curving into a smile as he nodded. "I'm glad you can see it. Things are never as bad as they seem."

She stared at him, the breath suspended in her chest. Was he trying to tell her something, or was it nothing more than an idle observation: a comment on the storm of the night before as compared to this glorious morning?

"I—I think I'll get a little sun."

"Just remember that you are getting twice as much as usual because of the reflection on the water."

She sent him a look of irritation. He had pulled off his own life vest and tee-shirt hours ago, just after they had eaten their combination breakfast and lunch. More than once the rays of the sun, catching on the gold disk around his neck, had nearly blinded her.

She removed her own vest, stripped off her top and shorts, and kicked out of her sandals. Propping her feet on the forward apron of the boat, she leaned back in her chair and tilted her hat over her eyes.

"Tiring business, fishing," he drawled.

She opened one eye. "What?"

"Pulling in all those bass must have been exhausting, still it's sweet of you to take a breather and give me time to catch up."

"Are you behind?" she asked, her lips twitching as she pulled her hat lower.

"You know very well I am," he growled, "by about two to one."

"Would you like to use my rod and reel?" she inquired.

As if to punctuate her words, the last striped bass she had caught, weighing nearly three pounds, slapped the water with a loud splash as it fought the wire-mesh holding basket let down on a line over the side of the boat.

"No, thank you," he answered, his voice dry.

Laughter bubbled up inside Kelly, then abruptly died away. What good was it to best him in this one small thing when he held the indisputable upper hand in everything that was important?

The sun beamed down. A hopeful mosquito whined around Kelly's face and she slapped at it. Silence hovered around them, broken only by the soft slapping of waves against the boat and the whirring sound as Charles cast his bait across the water again and again.

At a faint noise off to the left she opened her eyes to slits. There was another boat drifting toward their fishing place. On the far side of the clearing, it was a lightweight craft of green aluminum with two men in it. One of them was expertly plying a paddle so that they weaved silently through the trees.

She did not think Charles had noticed the new arrivals. He seemed intent on his fishing. In a moment, the two men would bring out their own fishing gear, attracting his attention. If she jumped up and began to yell, would they understand her? Would she be able to make sense before Charles stopped her? She could take a header out of the boat and swim toward the other men, but Charles would be after her in a flash. What would happen, however, if she first flicked on the trolling motor, and swung the handle to the left, guiding the bass boat into the trees? It would take him precious seconds to reach the front of the boat and turn it off, and that might be all the time she would need.

Before the thought had finished unreeling across her mind, she had surged to her feet, flicked the switch, turned the handle, and dived!

She swam underwater until her lungs were bursting, reaching, stretching, kicking with hard, desperate fury. She came up, but did not pause, drawing a long, rasping breath even as she settled into a strong, four-beat crawl. There was not time to look where she was going, no time for anything except the hard heart-straining effort. She could hear the beat of her own pulse in her ears, though the splashing as she clove the water drowned out the sound of the trolling motor. It had been three years since she had swum more than a lap or two up and down a municipal pool. The seconds ticked past, each of them an eternity. Her arms were growing heavy, and there was a growing ache between her shoulder blades.

She eased up enough to snatch a glance over her shoulder. It was an instant before she could locate the boat. It was lodged against the trees, floating free, empty.

Putting her head down, she redoubled her efforts.

Something touched the calf of her leg. She swerved, thinking it was an underwater snag or tree trunk. Then her ankle was caught in a grip of iron, and she was dragged under. She jackknifed, kicking free, but immediately a hard arm was clamped about her waist. With her chest aching as the air was driven from her lungs, she clawed for the surface.

She and Charles burst from the water together. Her eyes flew open as she dragged air into her lungs. He was so close to her she could see the flecks of rage in his eyes and the grim set to his mouth. His hold was merciless, but she had the advantage; it was he who for that brief instant was keeping them afloat. She brought her knee up. He twisted, catching it on his thigh. With that leverage, she drove the sharp point of her elbow into his chest, then with a catlike turn, drew back her fist, ready to drive it into his face.

He saw the blow coming. He rolled with it, pulling her with him. She caught her breath as her head went under the churning water once more, and then she was pushing, twisting, flailing, freeing herself only to be seized again. As she came up once, she opened her lips to scream for help, but his hand was clapped none too gently across her nose and mouth. For an instant, she could not breathe, and as a red haze rose before her eyes, the terrible fear shafted into her brain that he meant to drown her then and there. Her struggles became frenzied.

He released her, even supporting her for one fleeting instant before she struck out at him with the heel of her hand. He caught her wrist, jerking her against him, and they grappled once more, spinning, wrenching, heaving back and forth with their bodies intertwined in an oddly graceful water ballet that could not last. Kelly, her mind blank with despair, recognized that fact as she felt her strength failing while his seemed as steely and encompassing as when they had begun.

Abruptly his grasp loosened. She was free. It came so unexpectedly that she nearly sank as she neglected to tread water. She looked quickly at him, just barely within arm's reach of her. The startled expression on his face puzzled her, but she did not have time to think about it. Sweeping away from him, she began to swim again, pulling hard for the other boat. In that one moment of stillness, she had seen that it was leaving, had heard the rough curses of the men as they floated across the water. The two fishermen thought she and Charles were kids with no more sense than to stir up a good fishing hole by swimming in it.

"Kelly, my love, aren't you forgetting something?" Charles's voice as he called after her was provocative, with an undertone of warning that sounded an alarm in her mind. As she turned her head for air on an over-hand stroke, she glanced back, then stopped as if she had struck the lake dam itself.

In his hand Charles held aloft a scrap of material. Aqua-blue, with trailing strings that dripped with water, it was the top to her bikini.

At that moment, she heard the roar of a motor. Above its ear-splitting racket she could never be heard. It was the small power motor on the back of the aluminum boat. The men were scudding away under its noisy power. The opportunity that had seemed so bright moments before was gone. With dread in her eyes and her arms crossed over her breasts, Kelly swung to face Charles.

"How dare you?" she said, the words charged with choked fury.

"Easily, if I had thought of it, which, I am sorry to say, I didn't. It was an accident."

"Throw it here!"

He shook his head slowly back and forth. The anger had vanished from his face, and though its smooth planes were sternly solemn, the look in his dark eyes was bright. "You come and get it."

"I can't," she cried, her tone rising.

"Can't you?" he inquired, looking at the article of clothing he held as if he doubted its importance. Turning, he began to swim in the direction of the bass boat with long, easy strokes.

She sank her teeth into her bottom lip. "Charles? Charles!"

"It will be at the boat. You are coming, aren't you?"

"No!"

He stopped, swung to face her. After a moment, he tilted his head. "I would advise it. Any man who finds you clinging to a tree out here in that condition, like a mermaid in distress, may act first and ask questions later."

She watched in disbelief as he rolled with a lithe grace and began to swim once more. He was not going to give her top to her. He really wasn't. Her voice strangling in her throat, she yelled, "I'll kill you!"

"You're welcome to try—back at the boat."

The ferocity of the wrath that washed over her had no bounds. If she could have put her hands on him at that moment, she would have slain him without compunction. She felt on fire with disappointed rage and embarrassment. The blood boiled in her veins, and her skin was so red-hot it was a wonder that the water around her wasn't turned to steam. She tread water in an agony of indecision, knowing with frenzied certainty that the choice had already been made.

The anger was saving. It gave her the needed strength to kick forward and lift her painfully heavy arms in the strokes it took to cover the distance to the boat. Ahead of her, Charles had already reached it and was clinging to the side.

She swirled to a halt a few feet from him, covering her breasts with one arm as she tried with increasing tiredness to keep herself afloat. The water was dark and murky, but she was all too aware that with the sunlight shafting through it, the pale gleam of her flesh was visible. Holding out her other hand she said tightly, "All right. Give it to me."

"I'm not sure I should," he said judiciously. "You seem so much more reasonable without it."

"If you don't give that to me—" she began, then stopped with a catch in her voice as she lifted her chin high to keep her mouth and nose above water as she sank. She redoubled her treading efforts, but she could feel the ebb of the last reserves of her strength. Distress flared in her eyes.

"Charles, please," she whispered.

He had already started toward her. He caught her out-stretched hand, and with a powerful thrust against the water, brought her close enough to the boat to place it on the gunwale. She hung there for long moments with her forehead resting against the fiberglass side and her breathing harsh in her throat. It was a moment before she realized that Charles had released her and moved around to hold to the side of the boat behind her.

"Here," he said. "Put it on, and I'll tie it for you."

"No," she gasped.

"Don't argue, or I'll put it on myself."

The pale aqua top sailed over her shoulder, and spread out on the surface of the water before her with the right side up and the ties in the correct position. She scooped it up before it could sink and clasped it to her. She shivered a little as she felt Charles's warm fingers at her back, closing the slide, pushing the wet strands of her hair aside to form the bow. He was good at it, she thought wearily; no doubt the effect of practice.

"Are you all right?" he asked, his breath warm against the nape of her neck.

"I'm fine," she said in a stifled voice.

"Into the boat then. I'm going to give you a boost." She nodded her comprehension. An instant later, his hands were firm about her waist, and she was surging upward. It took the last of her energy to grab the side of the boat with both hands and pull herself high enough so that her weight could drag her inside. She lay on the bottom for a long minute, then turned, intending to help Charles. There was no need. He heaved himself up with the muscles bunching in his shoulders, then swung himself into the stern. With resentment burning inside her, Kelly watched as he strapped on his thin gold watch and gathered up the things he had taken from his pockets, a small, gold-handled knife, a handful of change, his billfold, and also her own billfold and car keys. A thorough man, Charles, and a swift one. He had taken the time to remove these things from his cut-off jeans, as well as turn off the trolling motor, before he had dived in after her.

Pulling herself up into her captain's chair, she collapsed. Her mind was numb with fatigue, and her hands shook as she pushed her fingers through her hair. Worse than the fact that he had captured her again was the ease with which he had done so, and his galling generosity in her defeat.

Behind her, Charles spoke. "I hate to tell you, but we lost our dinner. The cord that held the fish basket must have seen a few years. It broke when the boat went into the trees."

Kelly was saved from the necessity of answering as he cranked up the boat's motor, letting it idle in neutral. His voice, so cheerful and casual, grated along her nerves. She hated him, she told herself: She would pay him back for every moment of humiliation she had suffered at his hands if it were the last thing she did. She would personally see to it that his little game came to an end. He would never see a penny of the ransom money, never spend a dime. No matter what it cost her, she would get away from him and send the police. He would be arrested and thrown into jail, where she hoped he would rot the rest of his life!

"Excuse me?"

Without waiting for her compliance, he swung her captain's chair on its swivel and brushed past her, leaning to draw up the trolling motor. She glanced at him from the corner of her eye as he balanced with a knee on the front of the boat. One push would send him overboard again. She might have time to get back to the controls and push the boat into forward gear.

He turned his head, slanting her a quick glance as he switched the locking mechanism into place on the small motor. "I wouldn't, if I were you."

His eyes were steady and his face carefully straight, but a muscle twitched in his cheek as he tried not to laugh. Kelly turned her head, staring wide-eyed at nothing until he had taken himself back to the rear of the boat.

Damn the man, Charles-whatever-his-name-was! Angrily, she dashed tears of weariness from her lashes. She would show him. She would.

The sound of the outboard motor changed. They shot forward a few yards, then stopped, the motor idling as he pulled back on the throttle.

"Kelly, your life vest," he called.

She pushed herself erect, looking around her, realizing it must be behind her in the middle of the boat. Reluctantly, she swung, leaning hurriedly to pull it into her lap before she reached for the shorts and top beside it.

"Put it on," he said. "We wouldn't want to attract the attention of the lake patrol by being on the water without it, now would we?"

"In a minute, as soon as I get my clothes on," she snapped in unbearable annoyance, and immediately wished she hadn't as she heard his choke of laughter.

She sent him a murderous look and turned sharply around. Even if she had been nearly nude before him minutes ago, there was nothing funny about her urge to be completely dressed now, she told herself as she struggled into her clothes. He would pay, oh, how he would pay!

Back at the landing beside the catwalk, she snatched off her vest and threw it down on the seat, then clambered out of the boat. She did not look back as she ran along the walk and took the path to the house. Jerking open the screen, she crossed the veranda and entered the house, moving swiftly through the living room and down the hall. Inside her bedroom, she caught the door and slammed it shut with such violence it shuddered in its frame and the crash echoed through the house and across the water.

Kelly stood for long moments in the center of the room with her arms clasped around her and her eyes wide and unseeing. She took a deep breath, then with a shake of her head, moved toward the bathroom, intending to shower.

Abruptly she stopped as she heard the sound of the boat's motor once more. Listening intently, she could hear no sound in the house. Apparently, Charles had not followed her. Was that him in the boat? Was he putting it away in the boathouse? If so, how long would it take him?

Moving swiftly to the window, she drew the green-and-white drapes aside. It was the guard in the bass boat, though Charles still stood at the landing talking to the man. She would have a little time. With any luck, it should be enough.

She swung around, hurrying from the room. The door of the room Charles used was open. On the bed lay the clothes he had taken off earlier when he had changed. She gave them the barest glance before she slipped into the bathroom.

It was designed much like that connected to her own room. She went immediately to the medicine cabinet above the lavatory. Pulling open the door, she stood frowning. What she sought was not there. The shelves were empty of everything except the barest necessities.

In trembling haste, Kelly pushed the door shut, then began to draw out the drawers of the vanity table, pressing them silently closed again one by one. In the bottom drawer she found what she wanted, a first-aid kit. Taking it out, she snapped the latches and raised the lid. It was a well-stocked case a little larger than average. Besides an assortment of medicines, it contained a hypodermic syringe and a set of scapels. Ignoring these, she took up a small bottle containing pills she recognized from the days of her mother's terminal illness as sleeping tablets. Tipping four of them into her hand, she replaced the lid of the bottle, put it back into the box, and set the box into the drawer.

As she pushed the drawer shut, she heard the creak of the screen door on the veranda opening. Her heart lurched. She dived for the door, skimming through the bedroom and out into the hall, moving faster and more silently than ever in her life. The hall seemed endless, and then she was inside her bedroom with the door closed and locked behind her. She did not stop there, knowing that Charles might well demand that she open the panel and leave it open. She spun into the bathroom, and leaning over the tub, turned both taps wide open. For long, strained moments she stood listening. No one came. Nothing disturbed the quiet of the bedroom beyond the bathroom door. Only then, as she became convinced that she had done it, did she allow herself to sag in relief, allow her lungs to inhale deeply enough to still her ragged gasps for breath.

The afternoon passed slowly. Kelly took a leisurely

bath and rinsed her hair before changing into fresh clothing. Lunch time had come and gone, but she disregarded it. She was not hungry after her midmorning snack, and she had no wish to face Charles just now. That would come soon enough, but not until the feverish plans revolving and dissolving in her head were set in some kind of pattern. She heard the boat as the guard returned from wherever he had gone, heard Charles go out to meet him. She did not stir. Let them do as they pleased, so long as they did not bother her. She had to think.

In the end, she gave it up. She would have to watch her chance, go with the moment. So much depended on what Charles did or might do. Few would be the opportunities to use the pills. She would have to wait, control her impatience and anger, smile and be pleasant. It might even be that she would have to make her own opportunity.

She could not hide in her room forever, but still she put off leaving it, unwilling to go out and face Charles. Her temper had cooled, but she wasn't certain she could keep to her resolve to be polite if he made any reference to this morning's events. Despicable, arrogant, hateful man. He was everywhere she turned. It was so frustrating, she wanted to scream and throw things. Not that she ever had; she just needed some means of ridding herself of the pent-up tension of the last two days.

Two days. It seemed longer, much longer. She did not know if she could endure much more of Charles's presence, his control of her movements, his omnipotent ability to forestall her every effort to get away from him. Not the least of her irritation was the knowledge slowly making itself felt that the situation could be much more unpleasant for her if he wanted it to be. At no time had he exerted his full strength against her. There had always been the sense that he could have put an end to her struggles with him much quicker and more decisively if he had been willing to hurt her. When she struck him or tried to use her nails, he did not retaliate, preferring instead to confine her movements. His usual tactic was to prevent too much damage to himself while allowing her to tire. Even this morning, as she fought him in the water, half the time he had been supporting them both. There had even been that one moment, as much as she hated to admit it, when he had allowed her to rest long enough, after he had stopped her breathing to keep her from sounding the alarm, to renew her attack. If his sole aim had been to subdue her in the shortest length of time, he would only have had to hold her head underwater. She had tested his strength enough to know that, regardless of the fight she put up, he could have done it.

The knowledge, instead of earning her gratitude, only increased her ire. It seemed to belittle the threat she posed to him, somewhat like a strong man willing to handicap himself to assure an interesting fight.

All right, she was no match for him in speed or strength, but she still had the traditional woman's weapon. Men called it cunning, trickery, intuition, but a better word was intelligence. She could not be counted out yet. And if she had to stoop to methods that were not strictly fair and square, then so be it. There was nothing legal or just in his using his superior strength to keep her there against her will. He deserved what he got.

Several times during the afternoon she heard Charles moving about the house, going in and out. He sounded almost aimless, as if he were bored with his own company, or else disturbed about something. Once she got up and looked out the window, but he was only sitting in one of the lounges on the front veranda, staring out over the lake with his hands locked behind his head.

It was getting late, nearly dusk-dark, when she heard his footsteps in the hall. She expected them to stop at his room, but instead they continued, pausing outside her door. A knock came.

"Kelly?"

"Go away."

"Let me in."

She did not answer. She should have known he would not be deterred. The bedroom-door locks in the house were symbolic more than anything else. Constructed with a center hole in the outside knob, it was child's play to open them. Kelly heard his footsteps retreating, then coming back. A moment later, he stood in the open door. He slipped the carpenter's nail he had used to force the spring lock into his pocket and moved to stand at the foot of the bed.

"Very clever." She flicked him an annihilating look, but did not move from where she lay on her stomach with her chin propped on her folded hands.

"Thank you," he answered with perfect solemnity. "I have come at no small trouble to myself, as you know, to see if you are hungry."

"Not particularly."

"Well, I am. I have this inconvenient habit of eating at regular intervals. Some people who live on a more exalted plane, such as in a blue snit, may not need nourishment that often. I understand this, but still the question has to be asked."

"A what?" she inquired, diverted, but also resentful.

"A blue snit. It's on the order of sulking with muttered profanity."

Kelly tightened her lips to keep them from curving into a smile. For some ridiculous reason, she felt better now that he had come to her. Not that she intended to allow that to affect her. "I was not using profanity!"

"Ah, but you admit you were sulking?"

"No such thing."

"It doesn't matter," he told her, his tone soothing. "I'll take you out to the lodge across the lake to eat anyway."

Surprise brought her up from the bed. "You'll what?"

"Since we were cheated out of our fish dinner, I thought we might try the restaurant at the lodge. I'm told they do their specialty, catfish and seafood, well, but on no account should we order a steak."

"Who told you?" It was difficult to see in the twilight dimness of the room. The tenor of his words was calm and slightly amused.

"It might be more precise to say George was told—that's the fellow staying with the old gentleman in the guest cottage, in case you haven't been introduced."

"You know very well I haven't." His volunteering the information surprised her. She sat up straighter.

"No matter. About dinner—"

"Why?" she asked abruptly.

"Why the invitation? I told you, I'm hungry, and all this talk about fish has convinced me that's exactly what I crave."

If he was doing this for her sake, as some form of compensation, he had no intention of admitting it. "Aren't you afraid I might try to escape?"

"I'm fairly certain you will, but that's a chance I'm willing to take."

"Because you are certain you can stop me," she said flatly.

"I wouldn't say certain—"

"Only out of modesty, I presume?" she inquired with vinegary sweetness.

"And a hard-won conviction that it would be tempting fate. Besides, you may refuse to cross the room with me, much less the lake. I can carry you bodily a great many places, but I have better sense than to try it in a public eating house."

"Something you don't dare? I am overwhelmed."

"I'm sure. Do you want to go or not?"

The temptation to refuse was strong. Acceding to anything he asked was a bitter decision just now. She was not certain she could do it, and yet she knew capitulation would be the wisest course. Here might well be the opportunity she needed. Even if she were given no chance to get away, she might retrieve some of the ground she had lost this morning by her ill-advised attempt at freedom. She could practice being accommodating and, at the same time, prepare the ground for the moment when she would make a more determined and careful effort. None of these things could be accomplished as long as she remained cooped up in this room.

She took a deep breath. "I will be ready in half an hour."

✸ Chapter 7 ✸

She was as good as her word. Exactly thirty minutes later, they left the house. Kelly, a slender figure in a white sundress, the only thing suitable for evening she had brought with her, stopped at the foot of the steps. She glanced up at Charles.

"We can go in my car, if you like," she said.

He shook his head, an unfamiliar figure beside her in a gray business suit. "While you were dressing, I asked George to get out the speedboat. It will be quicker and, barring a storm or some other disaster, I believe I can get you to the lodge without mishap."

She moved ahead of him along the walkway. When they left the concrete for the muddy path down to the lake he took her arm. The heels of her white sandals made a tapping sound along the wooden catwalk. At the landing, she paused, waiting for Charles to go ahead of her down the steps, then give her a hand into the boat. She moved to the front, dropping into the cushioned vinyl seat behind the boat's windshield.

The cry of a loon came across the water, a haunting, mournful sound. For no good reason that she could think of, gooseflesh rose along Kelly's arms. She let her gaze rove the gathering darkness of the evening that was already blotting out the shapes of the trees, then looked to the man beside her. In the dim glow of the instrument panel, he seemed unaffected by the peculiar atmosphere of the lake at night. His face was calm and a little stern. She glanced away, drawing her shawl of silky gray-blue mesh closer around her shoulders.

Charles started the motor, then let it idle to a rich, rumbling purr. His voice was flat as he spoke. "There is something we had better get straight."

Kelly swung to face him. "Yes?"

"We will be going into a place where there will be other people. You may be tempted to involve them in what is going on here. I want you to understand, Kelly, that it would not be wise."

"Are you threatening me?" she inquired, her gray eyes sparkling with defiance.

"I'm telling you to think carefully about the consequences before you act. I'm sure you don't want to endanger innocent bystanders."

"You seem very sure of yourself. Has it occurred to you that you may be the one in danger?"

"Knowing how slow the average citizen is to believe an appeal for help, or to act on it when he is convinced, I doubt it. Still, I would like your word that you won't try anything."

"You would like me to put myself on the honor system, is that it?"

"That's the idea," he agreed quietly.

"And if I refuse?"

He reached to switch off the motor, then turned back to face her. "Then we don't go."

The look in his black eyes was implacable as he sat waiting for her answer with one arm resting on the steering wheel and the other along the back of the seat.

"What makes you think I won't give you my word, then break it?"

"If you were going to do that," he said, his mouth

curving in a grim smile, "you would not have warned me."

Was he wearing a gun under his suit coat? She could see no bulge that would indicate such a thing, but a good tailor could make it impossible to tell. She clenched her teeth together in painful indecision. What would he do if she tried to enlist the aid of the other diners? Muzzle her? Hustle her out? What if someone tried to stop him? How far would he go to insure that she remained his prisoner? Her imagination balked at picturing him as a killer, but there was the evidence of the exchange between him and George to cloud her judgment. Could she, in all conscience, risk forcing an answer?

"Kelly?"

"I won't try anything," she said on a long drawn breath. That did not have to mean that she would do nothing. There was still the possibility that she could pass a message someway, somehow.

"Thank you."

Kelly flung him a narrow look as he turned to flick the motor into life once more. It was odd, but the appreciation in his voice had almost sounded sincere.

The windshield of the speedboat provided protection from the blown spray and the swift wind of their passage. In an amazingly short time, they were easing up to the dock that jutted out from the lodge. The windows of the restaurant attached to the fisherman's hostelry glowed with light. Built out on piers over the water, it was not a large place, yet the number of boats bobbing around the dock and cars in the parking lot was an indication of the quality of the food.

It was cool inside and well lighted, as suited a place where fish bones, small, white, and hard to see, could be a problem. The walls were hung with nets ornamented with Japanese glass floats in purple, green, and amber. The tables were built of rough-cut, weathered wood. Ferns and trailing plants hung near the windows, and ceiling fans whirled overhead, stirring the rich smells of seafood gumbo and other dishes succulent with shrimp and oysters that perfumed the air.

They were shown to a table in front of a large picture window where they could look out over the gently lapping water. They studied their menus in silence. To Kelly, everything looked good. It may have been the delicious smells wafting from the kitchen, or the thought of how little she had eaten all day, but she was suddenly ravenous.

When they had placed their order and the waitress had taken their menus away, Charles leaned back. His dark gaze was warm as it rested upon the golden-brown waves of her hair brushed back from the oval of her face, and the soft apricot tint the sun had given her skin. The white of her sundress was a perfect foil for her coloring, while its square neckline gave her a demure look heightened by the shadows that lay in the depths of her gray eyes.

"Would it be a violation of my agreement to leave you alone, if I were to tell how lovely you look tonight?"

She did not want to antagonize him, not just now. With one finger, she traced patterns in the condensation forming on the outside of her water glass. "I suppose not. Thank you."

He continued to watch her. "You are quiet this evening."

"Am I?" What did he expect?

"You have been since this morning." He hesitated, then went on. "I didn't hurt you, did I?"

She sent him a flashing glance. "No."

"I'm glad, though I don't think the same could be said for your dignity, could it? I apologize for my actions. It seemed too good an opportunity to miss, and much more humane than what I originally had in mind."

"I can imagine," she said, the expression in her gray eyes shaded with irony, and something more.

He frowned, then made a small shrugging movement with his shoulders. "Can you? I suppose so. It would be too much to expect you not to be afraid of me."

"I'm not," she said with a swift lift of her chin.

"Then why do you flinch when I come near you? Why do you insist on trying to get away from me when I have told you that you are safe?"

"It's not that I'm afraid; just that I don't trust you."

He stared at her a long moment before transferring his gaze to the darkness of the lake beyond the window. "I don't suppose you can be blamed for that."

"If how I feel really bothered you," Kelly said, aware of the quickening of her pulse, "you would let me go."

"I can't do that."

"But why? I give you my word I am not a danger to you. I'm just a secretary, as I told you before, a friend of the judge's daughter."

"I know that, but it makes no difference," he said, his deep voice holding infinite patience.

"You know?" Kelly stared at him, thrown momentarily off balance.

"Not only did your identification check out, but I had a cable from the judge confirming your story."

"Then why—"

"You must know the answer to that."

"Because I saw George and the man with him?"

"And because there is a possibility you have been seen at the lake house by someone with a dangerous curiosity about the connection. The only way I can protect you is to keep you with me."

"Protect me! Isn't that a strange way of putting it?"

His dark eyes narrowed. "In what way?"

"Don't you mean it's the only way you can protect yourself?"

108

"Now where," he queried softly, "did you get that idea?"

The urge to accuse him, to pour everything she knew into hard and contemptuous words, brought an ache to her throat. Under the circumstances, however, that would only serve to put him even more on his guard. She lowered her lashes. "It's fairly obvious that you don't want the whereabouts of the elderly man with you known, since you kept me from leaving after I had seen him. I suppose you are afraid I can't keep my mouth shut, that I'll mention what happened to the wrong person."

"That's essentially correct, though not the full story."

She lifted her gray gaze to meet his dark eyes, caught by an odd inflection in his tone. "What is the full story, then?"

He hesitated, then shook his head. "I'm sorry, but it will be better if you don't know."

"Better for whom?" she demanded, her tone bitter.

"For you."

"You won't mind if I don't believe it? I don't think you're sorry at all, not for anything. I think you are enjoying every minute of this!"

"If it were possible to go back and start over, I would, in a minute, but since it's not, then yes, I'm enjoying it. I like having you with me, I like looking at you. It would be better if you could relax and accept it, but since you can't I'll just have to try to make the best of it."

"To find what entertainment you can in my feeble attempts to escape you!" she threw at him.

"I did apologize for this morning," he pointed out, his tone rasping.

She was prevented from replying by the arrival of the waitress with their first course, a steaming bowl of gumbo served with rice, French bread, and pats of butter in the shape of seashells. They ate in silence, though Kelly's appetite was not as sharp as it had been earlier.

While they waited for the entrée, they made stiff conversation about the decor of the restaurant, moving from there to a discussion of eating places in general. A chance remark drew a description of famous New Orleans restaurants and their specialities from Charles, which led to French cooking and its emphasis on the preparation of fresh, natural foods in season. Out of sheer contrariness, Kelly pretended to be skeptical that the last had anything to do with the cuisine of France. She had to be impressed, however, with the arguments Charles marshaled to convince her.

Their main course was a seafood platter featuring catfish, oysters, and butterfly shrimp fried in a batter delicately flavored with herbs, and with side dishes of french fries, hush puppies, and slaw. It wasn't fancy, but it was delicious, exactly what Kelly had craved. At last she leaned back with a replete sigh.

"Dessert?" Charles asked.

She shook her head regretfully. "I don't think I could."

"Shall we have coffee and liqueurs back at the house, then?"

She nodded, then gave him a veiled look. "I'll just go to the rest room before we leave."

He shook his head. "I can't let you do that," he said softly.

"What?" She looked at him with wide-eyed incredulity.

"You didn't really expect me to let you slip out the back, or take the time to write dramatic S.O.S. messages on the mirrors in blood-red lipstick."

"I wear lip gloss," she said, her voice even, "and I'm not even carrying an evening bag."

"I noticed. Where do you have the pencil hidden?"

"In my shoe," she quipped. The short stub was actually in her bodice, held by her bra in the best tradition of a movie heroine. She had come very near to secreting the sleeping pills there also, but decided the problem of removing them without being noticed was too great to be overcome while he sat across the table from her. With great regret that poison rings were out of fashion, she had left them behind. It was odd how little disappointment she felt at being prevented from using the pencil she had so carefully provided for herself. That may have been because she had not truly expected Charles to let her get away with it, or because her greatest hopes rested with the sedative she planned to administer.

"That must be uncomfortable," he commented, though his gaze alighted briefly on the neckline of her sundress. His lips curved into a grin as Kelly could not prevent herself from flicking a downward glance at her bodice to be certain the pencil was hidden from view.

Realizing what she had done, Kelly looked at him with pure dislike. "Shall we go, then?"

"By all means," he answered, and signaled for the check.

The moon was just rising above the tree tops as they left the restaurant. Bright and golden, one-quarter full, it sent a path of yellow light along the lake channel. Charles turned the speedboat into it, plowing the gilded water. As they gathered speed, the boat seemed to rise up out of it, skimming swiftly over the surface like a low-gliding night bird. In a few short minutes, they were slowing again, settling back into the water, sweeping in a wide circle that would take them into the dark interior of the boathouse. The noise of the inboard motor was suddenly louder, echoing off the metal walls, as they eased inside. Then abruptly everything was quiet as Charles turned the key. Kelly stirred, gathering her shawl around her, preparing to get out.

"Wait," Charles said, putting out his hand to touch her arm.

She opened her mouth to question him, then went

still, held by the listening intentness that gripped him. She stopped breathing for a long moment, but could hear nothing.

"All right," he said, his voice low. He rose, stepping from the boat to the platform that circled the inside walls of the boathouse. With an outstretched hand, he helped Kelly from the boat, then left her while he moved to the rear, pulling down the wide entry-port door and snapping the padlock that safeguarded it. Returning, he took Kelly's arm, and they walked quickly to the front entrance that opened onto the short pier connecting the boathouse to the shore. This he locked behind them before he joined her once more.

He did not start immediately for the house, but stood in the deep shade of the trees, slowly quartering the darkness with his eyes. Whether it was his tense alertness, or something in the soft and waiting silence of the night, Kelly did not know, but she felt her own heartbeat quicken. She turned her head this way and that, straining to see.

Suddenly a swath of light swept through the trees. At the same moment she heard a quiet hum that it took her a long instant to recognize as the sound of a trolling motor. A low-slung craft, painted a dark color that allowed it to blend with the night blackness of the lake, was ghosting toward them. On its bow was a spotlight that illuminated the shoreline, sending out a bold shaft of brightness that effaced the glow of the moon.

A quiet French expletive came from the man beside her. Then suddenly he reached out to encircle her waist with his arm. She stiffened, trying to draw away.

"For God's sake, not now," he said in a fierce undertone. "You can slap my face later."

Kelly allowed herself to be led from among the trees at a slow, lover's stroll. At his soft command, she allowed a musical chuckle to float on the gentle night air, joining his own laughter as if they shared a joke delicious in its intimacy. He kept his head close to hers, bending over her with tender attention as they moved up the path toward the house, apparently oblivious to the stabbing search of the white light. They were both aware of it, however, watching from the corners of their eyes as it traveled over the catwalk and past them along the water's edge, returning to play over the white walls of the dark and silent cottage. Then it came toward them; fast, noiseless, steady in its menace.

As they were snared in the brilliant glare, Charles swung her into his arms and kissed her. Kelly endured the searing pressure of his lips with her breath pent up in her chest. Unwilling, unable to resist, she clung to him in fear and impotent anger, and in a passionate despair that came from nowhere to curl around the edges of her mind and spread, achingly, to the region of her heart.

On a ragged, indrawn breath, Charles lifted his head. He stared down at her a long moment, then schooling his features to an expression of indignant wrath, turned to stare directly into the spotlight. Swinging back, shielding Kelly with the broad width of his shoulders, he moved on along the worn walkway to the sidewalk. He opened the screen door, urging her onto the veranda. For long seconds he stood watching the boat as it slid silently away, its light sweeping over the wire screen before it continued along the shore. Certain the boat did not intend to stop, he followed her into the house.

Kelly moved to the living-room window, holding the drape to one side while she peered out. She was in time to see the spotlight extinguished as the boat was lost to sight among the trees. Dropping the drape into place once more, she removed her shawl. With her hands clenched on the silken mesh, she turned to face Charles.

"What," she said distinctly, "was that all about?"

He sent her a smile that was a shade too casual. "I

expect it was a couple of boys out frog-gigging. The light blinds the big bullfrogs so they aren't so quick to jump. A homemade gig, made of a bent steel rod with the end bent into a hook, then filed to a point, gets them nearly every time. It's illegal because it's a cruel sport, but I used to do the same when I was growing up. There's quite a bit of white meat on a frog leg, a little like chicken."

"I know about frog-gigging: Peter and Mark used to go now and then. But I never saw them use such a powerful spotlight for it."

"Boats are equipped with all sorts of fancy extras like that these days." His tone was evasive and he did not meet her eye.

"Another thing, if you really thought that was all it was, what was the point of that charade out there?"

"Which charade was this?"

"You know very well. All that pretending to be my—that we were lovers!"

He snapped his fingers. "Oh, yes, I did promise to give you a chance to be avenged. Are you ready to hit me?"

The palm of her hand itched to do just that, but she controlled the urge. "I am trying to find out what is going on here, not play some kind of game!"

"But I've already told you."

"You don't expect me to believe that's all it was, a frog hunt?"

His gaze moved over her face, resting on the flush of anger that burned on her cheekbones. "It would help matters if you would."

"Well, I don't!"

"I told you earlier, Kelly," his voice with its trace of an accent dropping to a low note that sent a shiver along her nerves, "that it would be better for you not to know."

"I am, of course, supposed to accept your word without question?"

114

"I accepted yours."

"That's different," she cried. "You know who and what I am."

Pain flashed across his face so quickly she could not be certain she had seen it. An instant later, all expression had vanished. "I also said that I had to take what entertainment I could from the situation."

She did slap him then, a hard, open-handed blow that made her fingers ache, and left the side of his face red.

A muscle corded in his cheek. His voice soft, he asked, "Do you feel better now?"

She didn't. She wanted nothing so much as to cry, to scream, anything to relieve the painful pressure inside her chest. She clenched her hands into fists, incapable of making a coherent answer.

"I believe," he said slowly, "that we were going to have coffee and liqueurs before the excitement came up."

Coffee. Her brain fastened on the thought with calming desperation. This was the opportunity she had been waiting for. It was here. Now was the time.

"Yes," she said, taking a deep breath, her gray eyes never leaving his dark gaze. "If you will pour the drinks, I will put the coffee on to perk."

In the kitchen, Kelly got out the coffee pot and ran water into it. Setting the basket in place, she spooned ground coffee from the can, filling it to the level Charles usually used, then adding two more tablespoons for good measure. It would be strong, but it would need to be. She put on the strainer and glass-topped lid, then plugged the pot into the electric outlet near the sink. That done, she took down a pair of cups and their saucers, placing them on a small tray along with spoons, the sugar bowl, and a small jar of non-dairy creamer. Satisfied that everything was in readiness, she left the kitchen and went along the hall to her bathroom.

When she returned to the kitchen, the coffee was perking nicely, sending out its familiar aroma. From the living room came the strains of Haydn's *Farewell Symphony,* and she allowed herself a tight smile at the appropriateness of the choice. She leaned against the island cabinet, staring at nothing, waiting, aware of the four yellow tablets in the palm of her left hand.

The perking stopped. Kelly unplugged the pot, and lifting it with a steady hand, poured coffee into both cups on the tray, then set the pot back down. Taking an extra spoon from the drawer, she dropped the tablets she held into the cup on the right and gave it a brisk stir. She leaned over the sink to rinse the spoon under the running tap.

"What's taking so long?"

Kelly dropped the spoon with a clatter, jerking around. Realizing at once that he could not have seen what she was doing because her back was turned to the opening between the kitchen and dining room, she forced a smile. "It's ready now."

"Let me carry the tray for you," Charles said, coming forward.

"No! No, I can carry it," she said.

"I insist." He reached around her to put his hands on the handles of the tray.

To make an issue out of it might arouse his suspicions. Kelly moved aside with as much grace as she could muster, then preceded him into the living room. He placed the tray on an end table. Without too much haste, Kelly took her seat on the couch beside the table, picked up a spoon, and dipped creamer into the cup on the left. That took care of which cup was which well enough, since Charles used none in his coffee.

As she had expected, he picked up the cup containing the sleeping pills and, adding sugar, carried it to the easy chair across from the couch. There was a dark gold liquid in a thimble-sized glass on the table at his elbow, and another of the same for her on the table beside the coffee tray. Unable, suddenly, to bear watching _him_ _drink_ his coffee, Kelly reached and picked up the liqueur.

It was strong and fiery, and she grimaced as she swallowed. Setting the glass down, she sipped her coffee. The taste of the liqueur lingering on her tongue gave the coffee an added bite and it was all she could do to force it down her throat.

"What is this?" she said when she could speak, indicating her glass.

"Drambuie. Like it?"

"Not particularly."

"It's a little strong until you get used to it," he said.

"So is the coffee," she offered, glad to be able to slip in a word of warning in case he noticed the bitterness.

He drank from his cup, then sent her a smile. "Reminds me of the brew they serve up in New Orleans. The _bon vivants_ of the French Quarter used to say that for perfection it needed to be 'Hot as hell, black as the devil, strong as love, and as pure as an angel.' "

Kelly let her gaze touch the cup he held, then move on past him. "I'm not sure my coffee qualifies on all four counts."

"It's delicious," he said, saluting her with the cup.

Despite his overbearing ways, Charles was a man with many attractive qualities, not the least of them being his easy companionability at times like these, when she ceased to fight him. With his coat off and his tie loosened as he stretched at ease, he was devastatingly handsome, she had to admit, and yet he lacked the self-consciousness of most good-looking men. On occasion he could show great sensitivity, and an amazing empathy for what she felt and thought. What had he been trying to say earlier at the restaurant? That he would have liked to start over with her under different circumstances? The idea had a certain appeal. What would he be like if there were no senator, no George, no connection with organized crime?

117

What was she doing? The next thing she knew, she would be regretting what she had done, volunteering to remain in order to rehabilitate him. It was laughable, women's susceptibility to the appeal of a rogue. Or was it another aspect of the hostage situation, the reluctance to leave captivity because it had become comforting and familiar?

Kelly lifted her cup to her lips once more. Charles had half-finished his coffee and was sipping his Drambuie. He should be showing signs of sleepiness soon, after four tablets. Was that too many? Not enough for a man his size? What would he do if he began to suspect something was wrong before he passed out? Would he become violent? Why hadn't she thought of that before? She would have to be ready to jump up and run at his first movement.

"What are you thinking of?"

He was watching her, his eyes dark and considering. She met his gaze briefly. "Nothing."

"You must have been. You were frowning as if you had found a bug in your coffee, or else were hatching a new plot to give me gray hair."

"There's nothing wrong with my coffee," she said, and took another swallow to prove it.

"You were plotting then?"

"What else?" she inquired, sending him a bright smile.

He arched an eyebrow. "I'm beginning to feel like one of the villains in O. Henry's tale 'The Ransom of Red Chief.' You know it?"

"I think so," she answered, a gleam of real amusement rising in her gray eyes. "The story of the two con men who kidnap a ten-year-old boy who is a holy terror, and wind up paying his father to take him back?"

"He was an exhausting brat who did his best to wreak mayhem on them, had to be constantly amused, and robbed them of sleep because they were afraid of what he might do while they dozed."

118

"If you are comparing me to a brat," she began slowly.

"I'll have to agree that doesn't apply," he said, flicking her a glance where she sat curled into the corner of the couch, "but the rest is certainly apt."

"You know what to do to be rid of me."

"Yes, but unfortunately, real life is more complicated than fiction."

She stared at him, wariness creeping into her manner. She did not like the way he was watching her, the intent look of remorse and readiness in his dark eyes. Lowering her gaze, she swirled the coffee left in her cup. She was about to raise it to her lips, when she was caught by a sudden yawn. She smothered it with the tips of her fingers, then looked up as Charles emptied his cup and set it to one side before he came to his feet.

Alarm coursed along her veins as he swung toward her, but she could not seem to move. She felt the urge to yawn building in her chest again, and she looked in horror at the creamy coffee she held.

Charles leaned over her, reaching for her half-filled cup. At the last minute, she snatched it from his fingers. The warm brew sloshed over the side, soaking into the white cotton pique of her sundress. It scarcely seemed to matter. Her heart was pounding as Charles caught her wrist and forcibly removed the coffee cup from her hand.

"That's enough of that, especially since I don't know how much you put in it. At least you didn't drink your Drambuie. That combination of pills and liquor can be fatal."

"How—" she breathed.

He met her eyes briefly. "The oldest dodge in the world; I switched the cups while I was carrying the tray. As for how I knew, a window, such as the one over the sink in the kitchen, becomes a mirror at night with darkness behind it. Strive to remember that, my darling Kelly, the next time you decide to slip me a mickey."

She closed her eyes, as much to shut out the gentle mockery overlaid with concern of his smile as from need. Hopelessness washed over her, bringing a numbness so great that she did not protest as she felt him slip one hand under her knees and the other behind her back to lift her into his arms.

He carried her along the hall to her bedroom. There, he stood her on her feet while he whipped back the covers. As he turned back to her, his gaze moved over the brownish stain that marred the front of her dress. The next thing she knew, he had reached behind her, unzipped her dress, and was slipping the wide straps off over her shoulders.

"No," she exclaimed, fear cutting through the dazed distress of her senses.

"It would be a shame for your dress to be ruined."

Paying no attention to her clutching hands, he stripped the white sundress from her, leaving it in a pile on the floor as he picked her up and deposited her on the bed. He drew the sheet up, then sat down beside her, taking her hand in his. It was long seconds before she realized that his warm fingers were pressed to the pulse in her wrist.

He placed her arm across her waist, then sat staring down at her. Kelly kept her eyes resolutely closed. He would go in a moment, and she could be alone with her latest and most humiliating defeat.

Abruptly he bent forward to place his hands on either side of her pillow, lowering his lips to hers with a gentle, almost experimental pressure.

"Strawberries," he murmured. "You always taste of strawberries, and something more that is sweeter still."

It was her lip gloss but she did not intend to inform him of it. Slowly, she lifted her lashes. Her voice no more than a whisper, she said, "I hate you."

CAPTIVE KISSES

He got to his feet, his face like a mask as he moved toward the door. He paused with his hand on the knob to look back. "So you have said, not that I blame you. Sometimes, I don't like myself much, either."

❀ Chapter 8 ❀

Kelly let the screen door of the veranda swing shut behind her. She stood on the steps a moment with her hands pushed into the pockets of her jeans. The sun was shining. A light breeze swayed the Spanish moss on the trees and sent a soft rustling through the leaves of the dark green ceiling overhead. She frowned.

It was one thing to make up her mind, but something else to act on the decision.

She had awakened well into the morning. It seemed she had benefited from her enforced, dreamless sleep. Rested, if not refreshed, she had lain for some time thinking, endlessly mulling over what had taken place in these last few days. She had come to a few conclusions, none of them comforting.

First, she thought her failure to win her freedom was largely her own fault. She had let fear and the prospect of immediate freedom push her into hasty, ill-considered action. She would have been much better off to have waited, gaining Charles's confidence as originally planned, biding her time until his guard was down. As it was, she had only increased his wariness. It would take time to recoup the lost ground. Still, the effort had to be made. What other choice was there for her?

He was not indifferent to her; his attitude of the night before had made that plain. Whether it could be used to her advantage was questionable, but she had to try. If she could convince him that she had accepted her fate, that she was becoming content with his company, he might grow lax in his supervision. If she had little real hope of it happening, it was still her best chance. Then if the situation became desperate, his feelings for her might well tip the balance, meaning the difference between life and death.

Life and death. It was hard to believe, in the clear brightness of the morning, that the issue could become so clear cut. But she had not imagined that conversation she had overheard, nor the tense presentiment of danger that had hung in the air the night before when the boat with its spotlight had cruised past the house. Charles had tried to make light of it, to change the direction of her thoughts, and he had been successful for a time. On closer consideration, she wasn't deceived. He had been more tightly alert than at any time since the first day she had arrived. And this morning he was with George and the senator at the cottage. No doubt they were discussing the incident, plotting strategy.

Who had been in that boat? Was it the lake patrol, acting on some kind of information concerning Charles or his activities? Was it some other kind of police? That was the only supposition that made any sense, but surely any such authority would not have acted in a manner so certain to either put a criminal on his guard or else make him bolt. Maybe that was what they had wanted. Even so, it still didn't make sense. There had been nothing about the boat to indicate it was an official craft there in a legal capacity, and even Kelly herself had been affected by something sinister in its activities.

There was another possibility. If the senator was sufficiently important, if he had been carried across state lines, then his kidnapping became a federal crime, under the jurisdiction of the FBI. If that were the case, however, wouldn't there have been a big commotion about it in the newspapers and on television? Charles had said they had been in residence at the lake house for a week before her arrival on the scene. She would have noticed a case like that in the news before she left. The only front-page issue she could remember reading about was the bribery and corruption scandal growing out of the last election. One of the top politicians in the state was supposed to come to trial on charges stemming from it when court reconvened in less than a week now, and the media had been having a field day with it. It was remotely possible that these local events had overshadowed other items to the point where they might have gone unnoticed.

The slamming of the door drew her attention toward the cottage. From her bedroom window earlier she had seen Charles making his way in that direction. Now it was with dread as well as anticipation that she saw a man leave the front porch and move toward the catwalk.

It was George who stepped from among the trees. He carried a fishing rod in his hand, but as he scanned the surface of the lake he had nothing about him of the relaxed content of the fisherman. On sudden impulse, Kelly moved down the steps, setting out on the path that would take her to the water's edge.

"Good morning," she called when she was in hearing distance, though she kept her voice as low as possible.

The man turned. "Good morning."

Though there was a certain reserve about him, the hefty guard had smiled. Kelly decided to take this as an invitation to join him on the catwalk.

"Nice day," she offered as she drew nearer.

"Yep."

He was not exactly a talkative sort. "Where is Charles?"

The guard tilted his head in the direction of the cottage, as she had expected. "He'll be out in a minute, now that you're up."

"He—is a strange man." She didn't know what she hoped to gain by this one-sided conversation, but she persevered.

"Mr. Duralde? I wouldn't say that exactly."

Kelly felt a quickening along her veins. Duralde. She had his last name. A vague memory flickered, then faded. She let it go. "Any man who does what he's doing can't be ordinary."

The guard sent her a straight look. "He told you about it, did he?"

"A little." It would not do to pretend to know too much.

"Well, it does take guts, I'll have to hand him that."

Carefully, she formed her next question. "Why do you suppose he's doing it?"

"Doing what? Watching after the old guy? First off, because of the way old man Duralde, his dad, got it, and second, maybe because he gets tired of the rat race."

"That would be it," she agreed with a nod she hoped looked knowing.

"He's a throwback, you know, like the old planters that used to stay out on their land without seeing a soul nine months out of the year, then the other three go into New Orleans and raise merry hell, slice each other to ribbons, or blow each other's brains out on the dueling ground."

"He—lives above New Orleans, doesn't he?"

"That's right. Takes care of the whole shooting match; cane fields, soybeans, oil wells, cattle, you name it, by himself. It's like a regular town; and him the mayor, doctor, and fire chief rolled into one."

"He didn't say much about it," she said. "I suppose it's a big place?"

"I should say so. Back when his dad was alive and involved up at Baton Rouge, they had their own railroad spur and post office."

Kelly felt a rising excitement. She was close to something important; she could sense it. George was garrulous enough, it seemed, as long as he thought she had been told more than she had.

"Charles's father—" she began.

"There you are, Kelly. I've been wondering when you were going to get up so I could have breakfast."

She turned her head sharply to see Charles lounging at the end of the catwalk. As much for the benefit of the guard as for Charles, she gave him an offhand good morning.

"Come along and stop distracting George. He's hopeless enough with a fishing rod without someone like you at his elbow."

"Aw, Mr. Duralde," the guard protested.

Charles's dark gaze did not waver as he smiled at Kelly. For all the humor and the implied compliment in his words, it was a command.

"You shouldn't have waited for me," she said.

"And eat alone when I could have your charming company? Unthinkable. Besides, you are better at frying bacon."

Keep it light. That seemed to be Charles's attitude toward her this morning. It had certain advantages, even Kelly could see that; and if it would get them over the hump of their first meeting after the fiasco of the night before, then that was all to the good.

"Duralde," she said with an effort at airiness as she walked beside him back toward the house. "At least I know your last name now."

"Does that help?" He slanted her a quick look from the corner of his eye.

"I think it does."

126

"That's good then."

"I still don't know why you didn't want to tell me." She had a good idea but it might be best to affect innocence.

"I thought you might be the type to read post-office wanted posters, but apparently not."

Was he attempting to disarm her by making a joke of the truth? She would not put it past him, and yet, the more she tried to picture Charles Duralde as a killer, the more fantastic it seemed. "I—I'll have to mend my ways."

He made no answer as he held the screen door for her, then followed her into the house. They went straight to the kitchen. Kelly took out the bacon and began to peel the strips apart, placing them in the electric skillet. Charles got out the makings for toast. It was as if they were a couple long married with a set routine, Kelly told herself. The only difference was her acute awareness of him as he moved about the homey task with a kitchen towel tucked into the top of his jeans. He handled himself in the kitchen with brisk, masculine efficiency, as if cooking were a neutral task neither male- nor female-oriented, one that had to be done and therefore should be completed with the greatest dispatch. It was doubtless because he was single, used to doing his own cooking, and because he knew that she would refuse if ordered to perform such menial chores alone, that he pitched in so willingly. If he ever married, he would probably sit back like most other men and expect his wife to do everything.

Perhaps she was assuming too much? Maybe he was already married? Just because he had taken her in his arms, because he had not refuted any of the bachelor pursuits she had suggested as his interests, did not mean that he had no wife. There was no ring on his strong brown hand but some men did not wear them.

It didn't matter, naturally, but she was curious. Her mother used to say that if she wanted to know something the best way to find out was to ask, and if the man who was keeping her prisoner gained the impression that she was becoming personally intrigued with him, wasn't that what she wanted?

"Tell me something, Mr. Duralde—"

"My name is Charles."

"Charles then. Is there a Mrs. Duralde? Someone with whom you usually share these little domestic duties?"

He gave her a swift glance as he slipped the toast pan into the oven and turned to the refrigerator to take out a can of frozen orange juice concentrate. "You mean my mother?"

"You know very well I don't!"

"Then you want to know if I'm married. I wonder why?"

"No reason," she said with a slight shrug.

"How disappointing. The answer is no."

Kelly realized belatedly that she should have been more provocative about her reasons, should have smiled at him, lifted a brow, anything except retreat into sullenness. Or would that kind of behavior, coming so soon after the night before, have made him suspicious? The art of seduction was something she knew little about. It was going to require some careful thought.

A few minutes later, she turned to the dish cabinet for a platter for the bacon just as Charles was reaching for juice glasses. She brushed against him for a brief instant. This time, before stepping back, Kelly remembered to allow her lips to curve upward momentarily. The effect was worthwhile. For a long instant he stood still, a suspended look in his dark eyes as they rested on her face.

Abruptly he moved aside. "After you."

She was not certain whether to be elated or disappointed that he held himself away from her, well beyond the range of touch, accidental or otherwise.

Over the breakfast table, Kelly racked her brains for something to talk about. She could come up with little other than the most trite of commonplaces. It would not do, she thought, to mention the things George had told her. It was likely to bring about a crisis, causing Charles's wrath to descend on the man's head, which would, in turn, prevent her from learning more from the guard. More than that, it would give him the impression that she had been snooping, a direct contradiction of the picture of fatalistic resignation she wanted to create.

That did not prevent her from thinking about what she had learned. What in the world had George meant by saying that Charles took care of the whole shooting match? He had made it sound like some kind of giant farming operation or business conglomerate. What had that to do with a Mafia operation? It made no sense.

Duralde. The name plagued her. It could be she had heard it mentioned along with those of some of the other figures in the state who operated outside the law, men reputed to be crime bosses of high standing. If so, she could not pinpoint when or how.

Kelly washed the dishes, and Charles dried them and put them away. Afterward, she went along to her room to put it right. There she rinsed the coffee stain from her dress that she found soaking in her bathtub. Looking at it brought the night before more vividly to mind than was comfortable. Her gray eyes were shadowed as she hung the sundress on a hanger to drip dry.

When there was nothing else to be done in the house, she picked up her book and wandered out onto the veranda. She had not been in her place in the porch swing for long before Charles emerged from the house with a news magazine in his hand. He pulled a lounge away from the wall and stretched out in it, but did not open his magazine immediately. Leaving it on his lap, he locked his fingers behind his head, his gaze moving to rest on her absorbed face.

"Is reading all you do in the way of recreation?"

She glanced up to shake her head, allowing herself a smile with a hint of warmth as she met his gaze. "I play tennis now and then with one of the girls at the office, and sometimes I swim."

"I suppose you live in one of those huge apartment buildings for singles, complete with tennis courts and saunas?"

"As a matter of fact, I live in a Thirties Modern house with a nice old lady who turned her home into a duplex in order to have the extra income."

"You help her listen for prowlers, and she mothers you?"

"I walk her spaniel, she cooks dinner for me on Sunday, and the dog listens for prowlers for both of us!"

"A charming picture. What did she think of you coming down here alone for your vacation?"

"If she knew about it, she would be properly horrified, but she doesn't. She's spending the month with her son in the Ozarks." There was no point in not telling him the truth. If she had intended to claim the protection of her landlady, she would have mentioned her special interest long before now, when he had first asked about her friends and relatives.

"Is she the one who keeps all the young men away?"

"Which young men are they?"

"All those who should have swept you off your feet and down the aisle before now."

"Oh, those young men. She doesn't encourage them to come around, if that's what you mean. She waits up for me when I go out, too, and bangs on the wall if they play the stereo too loud when they come inside."

"A paragon. I wish I could meet her."

"She would make short work of you," Kelly told him, shielding her expression with her lashes as she considered the implications of his last remark. Was he suggesting in a subtle way that he would like to see her when this thing was over, if it was ever over?

"That remains to be seen; I'm at my best with older women," he informed her.

"That explains it, then!"

He sent her a quelling look. "I refuse to pursue that remark, since I left myself wide open for it. I'll ask instead how your foot is healing?"

"It's fine, practically well." She followed his lead without hesitation, just as happy herself not to be called on to explain her impulsive comment on his technique with women, something she had called into question once before. She had good reason now to know there was not a thing to fault.

"No problems after getting it wet yesterday?"

Was it only yesterday? "None."

"That's good."

A silence fell. In the quiet, the buzzing of a fly inside the screen wire of the veranda was loud and droning.

"I should thank you for taking care of my dress last night. The coffee came out without any problem."

He flicked a glance at the flush that was creeping across her cheekbones, then returned his regard to the fly now hovering in a sunny spot on the floor. "I could say I was happy to do it, but you would probably misunderstand."

"I—don't believe so," she told him, then went on, choosing her words with care. "I've been thinking about last night. If there was ever going to be a time when I wasn't—safe here, with you, it should have been then. You left me alone, even after what I tried to do. I've come to the conclusion that, if you are willing to offer it again, I will accept your word, and try to relax and be at ease during the days left of my vacation here with you."

"Extraordinary."

She looked up, startled. "What?"

The look in his eyes as he studied her was reflective, measuring. "You say that almost as if you mean it."

"Don't you believe me?" With a superhuman effort, she injected a wry note into her voice.

"I would like to, but past experience doesn't encourage me to bring out the champagne, not yet."

"You are getting old and cynical before your time," she accused. Keep it light, at all costs.

"If that's so, you will have to shoulder a part of the blame."

"I couldn't possibly. I'm much too exhausted from trying to find a way to get away from you."

"Now there's a reason I can believe, especially if you are half as tired as I am from trying to see that you don't."

"When you see how lazy I mean to be you will have no doubts."

He stared at her a long moment, and it seemed the darkness of his eyes deepened to a jet blackness. "Be sure, Kelly," he said softly. "We called a truce once, and you broke it. Do it again, and the results will be on your own head."

The expression on his face sent panic skittering along her nerves. He might complain of weariness and the strain of watching her, but it was only words. They meant nothing, any more than her own did in the same vein. She must not forget that, not for a moment.

They were distracted by a boat on the lake. A dark brown fiberglass craft built low in the water for the fast speeds of water skiing, it carried two men past the house and cottage at a pace so slow it threatened to stall the motor.

"Do you suppose that's the same one that came by last night?" Kelly asked, keeping her voice low though there was little danger that the two men could hear.

"I don't know," Charles answered, but his dark gaze followed the slow-moving craft.

Kelly leaned to see the catwalk. George must have gone back into the cottage. He was no longer in sight.

132

For no good reason that she could think of, she was glad.

It was an endless day. The minutes and hours crept by with funereal slowness. Because of Charles's presence it was difficult for her to concentrate on her book, difficult to become involved enough in the story to grow oblivious of time. Her attention was diverted every time he turned a page of his magazine, every time he looked up to scan the lake or glanced in her direction. She was more conscious of him, in fact, than she liked. She would have given much to be able to ignore him. It would not have advanced her program one iota, but would have done much to steady her nerves.

Since they had eaten a late breakfast, they had a late lunch and a light one. Charles helped to clear away the litter of cold cuts and relishes, then, his manner a little more casual than the occasion seemed to call for, left the house. Kelly, stifling a sense of pique at being alone that even she recognized as unreasonable, returned to her book.

She could not concentrate even when Charles was not there. After almost two hours of trying, she gave it up and tossed the volume to one side. A frown between her eyes, she stared at the cottage. The urge to break up the conference going on in there was strong. What were they discussing? The boat that had passed before lunch? Her new attitude? Or was Charles testing her, trying to see what she would do if left with time on her hands and no apparent supervision?

It was possible, of course, that he was tired of her company. They had been together almost exclusively for the better part of three days. Maybe he felt the need for masculine conversation? He didn't strike her as one of the boys, and he had said himself that he preferred his privacy rather than staying in close quarters with the other men, but there had to be some explanation for him leaving her by herself.

It was growing hot on the veranda as the sun leaned

toward the west, but Kelly did not like the idea of retreating into the closed-in walls of the house. The
water of the lake, ruffled now and then with long, slow
waves caused by the wake of a boat far out in the
channel, looked inviting. What would Charles do, she
wondered, if she decided to go swimming? She could
see no reason why he should object. He had used the
floating raft often enough.

A short time later she left the house wearing her bikini under a short jacket of white terry cloth and with
her feet thrust into sandals. At the point were the path
leading down to the lake left the concrete walk between the house and the cottage, she paused. She could
leave Charles to find out what she was doing himself,
or she could tell him. What better excuse than the last
did she need for interrupting his meeting?

A daring smile twitching at the corners of her
mouth, she continued along the walk.

"Charles?"

She did not quite dare to go all the way to the door,
but called to him from the steps to the porch of the
cottage. Standing with her hands pushed into the hands
of her toweling jacket, she awaited developments.

They were not long in coming. Charles emerged
from the house with a scowl drawing his brows together. "What is it?"

"I wanted to tell you I was going swimming." With
her head held high, she met his gaze squarely. Behind
him, the older man they called the senator had come to
the screen door. Kelly gave him a smile and a quick
nod.

Charles flicked a glance behind him, and his lips
tightened. Without being obvious about it, he shifted,
cutting off her view of the door. "Is that all?"

"Yes, except that you are welcome to come with me,
if you like."

"A magnificent concession, all things considered," he
drawled. "How could I refuse?"

"Would you like me to wait for you?" she inquired, forcing her lips to curve into a smile.

"By no means. I'll join you in a few minutes."

There was nothing for her to do except turn and leave. As she made her way down to the lake, she stared down at the path snaking away under her feet. Charles thought she should recognize the senator, just as he had expected her to recognize his name. That she could do neither was maddening. If she knew those two things, she was certain she would have the key to what was taking place here. She would know the answer, good or bad, once and for all.

She left her wrap hanging on one of the low posts at the end of the catwalk. With a clean dive, she went into the water and swam slowly toward the floating platform. When she reached it, she touched it with her hand as if greeting an old friend, then turned to her back. She floated, staring up at the sky overhead that was colored the soft, heat-faded blue of late summer. On the surface, the water was like a warm bath, though now and then she drifted through shafts of coolness caused by deep, shifting currents or the upward spiraling of underwater springs. Now and then a small fish, a bream or a perch, nibbled at her side, but she knew from long experience that they could not hurt her. The sun dazzled her eyes and she closed them, letting herself go, allowing her thoughts to scatter, mindlessly permitting herself to be borne by the water.

It came seeping into her consciousness then, the knowledge of where she had heard the name Duralde before. She knew, though what good it would do her she could not decide.

Water was a good communicator of sound. She heard the splash as Charles struck the lake, and the roiling of the water as he made for the platform. Turning to her stomach, she struck out, setting a course that would allow her to join him there.

The platform, or raft, of thick, rough-cut lumber,

dipped on its anchor chains as Kelly hauled herself up on it. Charles, sitting on the edge, extended his hand to grasp her arm. Off balance, not expecting the extra help, she toppled against him. The moment was not of her making, but it would serve.

With a breathless sensation in her chest and laughter in her gray eyes, she lay in his arms. "Sorry," she murmured.

The muscles of his biceps tightened, and the bronze of his skin turned a shade darker. With her shoulder pressed against his chest she could feel the hard beat of his heart. "My pleasure," he said, his voice rough.

Without hurrying, she pushed herself upright to sit beside him, kicking her feet in the water.

Aware of the acceleration of her own pulse, Kelly looked away out over the lake. She thought of one or two things to say, but they bordered on being too flirtatious. It would not do to launch at once into the subject uppermost in her mind. She compromised with a white lie. "I hope I didn't take you away from anything important."

"It didn't matter," he answered, his tone smoother now. "The older man you saw in the door at the cottage has been wanting to get a closer look at you ever since you came, but especially since I told him this morning about the way you doctored my coffee."

"Oh?" She wasn't too sure she liked that.

"Don't get on your high horse. He just wanted a glimpse of the woman who has been keeping me so busy."

"I'm always happy to provide amusement," she said, her tone even.

"As far as that goes, I think the laugh was on me. I was so certain, you see, that this would be a nice, quiet place to stay, without distractions or disturbances of any kind."

She was a disturbance and a distraction to him; that had a promising sound. Now would be the time to see if she couldn't upset him a little more. "I've been thinking. There was a man named Duralde who used to go fishing now and then with Judge Kavanaugh. The judge usually kept his fish fries for his cronies and business associates separate from his outings with his family, so I don't believe I ever met this man, but, I remember Mary mentioning him. I had the impression he was an older man, the judge's age. If I'm correct, he must have been your father."

"That's right." Charles spoke in a quiet timbre, giving nothing away of his feelings.

"He was a man of influence: of what kind, I'm not sure. I believe he was killed some months ago in an accident." She was not certain she would have remembered the last point if George had not mentioned something about the way Charles's father had died. He had seemed to hint there was a mystery about it, but if so, there had been no details in the small news item she had read.

He did not reply. She turned her head to look at him, but his gaze was fastened on the far shoreline, his features grim and unreadable. She didn't know what she had expected; anger perhaps, or else some indication that she had stumbled upon an important piece of the puzzle. As it was, she was left with no more than a vague idea of how the judge had come to lend his place on the lake to Charles.

"Well?" she said, her patience at an end.

"Well what?" He swung to face her then. "If you are waiting for me to enlighten you further, you will wait a long time. I thought you were going to relax and stop tormenting yourself like this."

"I can't stop thinking about it, and I don't see how you can expect it. I'm not stupid."

"No," he said, the expression in his dark eyes suddenly wry, "and I don't know whether to be glad or sorry."

❦ Chapter 9 ❦

The sun set in orange splendor. It flung great swatches of crimson and mauve across the western sky, giving the reflective waters of the lake a pink-and-blue opalescent sheen. The trees on the horizon were a ragged black line, while nearer at hand there was a silvery lilac gleam on the undersides of the leaves of the live oaks.

Kelly watched the display from the veranda. Its melancholy beauty touched a somber chord inside her, increasing, rather than lightening, the numb depression that gripped her.

What was the matter with her? What had become of her anger and outrage, her fine, spitting defiance? Had hopelessness made her a coward, or was it simply that such a state of high emotion could not be sustained without the fear that had fueled it? For she had to admit that she was no longer afraid of Charles. His nearness troubled her, and she was always intensely aware of him, but he did not affect her anymore with that rush of painful apprehension. It was peculiar, as though exposure to constant danger had given her a contempt for it. She would go on fighting him, no mat-

138

ter how devious the manner, but her heart was no longer in it. Her heart?

It was with a sense of relief that she caught sight of movement among the trees. It was George, walking quietly from the cottage to the boathouse in the deepening twilight. As she watched, he entered the building. Within a few minutes, there came the sound of the entry port opening, followed by the rumble of a motor. The judge's bass boat eased from the shelter. The throbbing noise of it changed as it was put into gear, then it glided away across the glassy waters of the lake, heading without haste for the channel.

There was no point in even wondering where he was going. Kelly turned back into the house.

Preparing dinner was a means of passing time, as well as a possible way to endear herself to Charles. The way to a man's heart was through his stomach, the old saying went.

Hearts again. She had the subject on the brain. With a shake of her head, she began to comb the kitchen for the ingredients to make red beans and rice.

A little ham, a little sausage, a bit of hamburger, onions, garlic, celery salt, pepper, tomato sauce, parsely, thyme, and the contents of a can labeled kidney beans were soon bubbling in a pot. With that out of the way, Kelly put on the rice, taking great pains since she wanted it to turn out light and fluffy, as good rice should be. Red beans and rice, a south-Louisiana favorite, was a meal in itself. All it needed as a complement was a green salad. She rubbed the salad bowl with garlic, then washed lettuce and pulled it apart. Cutting up a handful of small and juicy ripe cherry tomatoes, she put them in, then set the salad in the refrigerator to crisp. Next, she made iced tea for herself; Charles could have wine with his meal if he wanted it, but she intended to keep a clear head.

It was just as well that she had gone to so much effort. About the time she had everything under control,

Charles strolled into the kitchen. He leaned in the doorway a moment, watching her as she moved back and forth. He had come from the direction of the bedrooms in the back of the house where he had been showering, taking his own good time about it. Pushing away from the door frame, he lifted the lids of various pots and pans, sniffing appreciatively. Before he could ask, she told him what she was cooking.

"Smells delicious. I'm starving."

"Everything is ready; it only needs putting on the table."

"Is there enough for three?" he asked, sending her a quick look.

"More than enough. Were you thinking of inviting your friend in the guest cottage?"

"That's right."

"As far as I'm concerned, he's welcome," she said, her gray gaze clear. The senator would be alone since George, so far as she knew, had not returned.

"I had in mind something more on the order of a tray for him."

"All right." She turned to the cabinet to take down an extra plate.

When the tray had been arranged, Charles picked it up, and threading his way around the dining-room table, started down the hall.

"Where are you going?" She smiled a little as she waved a hand toward the front door. "If you will remember, the cottage is that way?"

He stopped and turned back. "I know," he said, his voice quiet, so soft she could barely hear it. "But our friend isn't."

The truth dawned on Kelly as she watched his broad back disappear down the hallway. Under the cover of darkness, while she was busy in the kitchen, Charles had spirited the man he called the senator into the house, establishing him in one of the back bedrooms. Why? Did it have anything to do with the fact that

George was not there to guard him? Or was the connection with the boat with the spotlight the night before? The questions were bothersome, but she left them unasked, knowing she was unlikely to receive direct answers.

They ate in silence. Once Charles, in an odd reversal of his usual habit, rose from the table and opened the drapes at the windows across the front of the house before returning to his chair. Despite the fact that the house was too high above the water level to permit anyone on the lake to see inside, and the unlikelihood of anyone else being in a position to look in, it made Kelly uncomfortable. She did not like knowing that they were illuminated under the light above the table as surely as actors under a spotlight on the stage.

Once she met Charles's gaze across the width of the table, puzzlement in the depths of her eyes. The smile he gave her was warm with reassurance. There was also a caressing quality about it, as if he enjoyed the picture she presented with her scooped-neck tank top over her jeans, her cheeks flushed from the heat of cooking, and the soft waves of her freshly shampooed hair drawn back from her face with a blue ribbon.

She lowered her lashes, staring at the food on her plate, pushing it this way and that. Swallowing hard on the tightness in her throat, she looked up again. "Charles—"

"Not now, Kelly. Someday I will answer anything you care to ask, but not now."

The quiet tone of his voice sent a flutter of alarm along her nerves. The muscles of her stomach tightened, and she knew a prickling sensation at the base of her neck, as though she were being watched. The stillness in the dark regard of the man across the table seemed to form a pact between them, one completed as she nodded in acceptance of his terms. And yet, his concession did nothing to ease the edginess that held her in its grip.

Kelly got up from the table at last, and taking her plate and utensils, carried them to the sink. She rinsed them under running water, then put the stopper in the sink to catch hot water for the dishes. Charles crossed the room behind her, bringing his own plate and glass, as well as the bowl of rice.

Kelly gave him a quick glance. "I can manage alone. You don't have to help."

"If you do it by yourself, that means it will be twice as long before you can join me." As she started to protest, he added, "And I prefer to have you with me as much as possible."

There was something different about him tonight. He was controlled as always, but still there was a suppressed recklessness in his eyes, as if he chafed under the bonds of civilized behavior. As he stood close to her, she could sense the emanation of vibrant life electrifying in its strength. She had the feeling that if she made the slightest move toward him, or even if she stood still so near him, he would take her in his arms without regard for the consequences. It was with a great effort that she forced her stiff body to turn away, to reach for the dishwashing liquid and turn off the still-running water.

The moment passed, but it could not quite be put behind them. When they had finished in the kitchen and retired to the living room, he poured glasses of white wine for them both, then put a stack of records on the stereo, most of them Mrs. Kavanaugh's instrumentals from the forties. Smiling blandly, though with a devilish glint in his eyes, he drew her to her feet and out into the clear center of the floor. They danced to the slow and sentimental music as in a trance, moving in perfect unison. His hold was light and yet firm, his lead without hesitation. As one, they let the music guide them, relinquishing cerebral control for the ancient pleasure and grace of body rhythm.

His arms were a haven, immensely comforting, affecting her with a feeling of belonging that disturbed her. She drew back once to stare at him, a half-smile without coquetry curving the pure lines of her mouth. On a harsh, indrawn breath, he drew her back against him.

Still, even in their self-absorption, they were neither of them quite oblivious of the still darkness of the night beyond the uncovered windows.

The record changed. The soft melodies to which they had been moving were replaced by the faster tempo of a disco album, one Mary must have left behind. The sound was louder and more frantic. It seemed to vibrate through the house with a self-perpetuating tension. Keeping up with it, and with Charles, was an exciting challenge. It was also tiring and thirsty work. Kelly was glad when the last pulsing beat died away and she could catch her breath while they sipped their wine.

Charles drained his glass, then stood turning it in his hand. "Kelly," he began.

She flicked a quick glance from the windows to the hallway that led to the back bedrooms. Suddenly, she could not stand to be where she was another minute. She set her wine glass down with a sharp click. "Shall we go outside for a little air?" she interrupted.

"I don't think—" he began, but she had already surged to her feet. Moving to the door, she pulled it open and stepped out into the deep-shadowed stillness of the veranda.

The moon was rising, a sickle moon that seemed to have its lower horn caught on the trees. It shed its pale radiance over the water, turning it into a silver mirror framed by the spiky black forms of the trees. She turned her footsteps in the direction of the porch swing. By the time she had reached it, Charles had closed the front door she had left standing open and moved to where she was, standing ready to take a seat beside her.

Kelly moved over to give him room. He stopped her

with a touch on her shoulder, dropping down close beside her. In an effort to dispel her tenseness, she inhaled, filling her lungs before she let the air out slowly. There seemed to be a freshness in the night breeze that had been missing before, an intimation of fall.

"Does it seem cooler to you tonight?" she asked.

"A little," he agreed. He stretched his long legs out, setting the swing into motion, while at the same time he extended one arm along the seat at her back.

"In less than two weeks the summer will be officially over."

"So it will."

"Four more days, and I am supposed to be back at work."

"You would like to know if there is any chance you will be there?" he queried, his voice coming low beside her.

"Something like that." She kept her tone quiet and reasonable with an effort.

"You can leave here tomorrow, if you like."

She turned to look at him in the dimness lit only by the glow from the windows. "Do you mean it?"

"I'm not in the habit of saying things I don't mean."

The payoff must have come then, or else he was expecting George to bring it with him when he returned. "I suppose you will be leaving too?"

"Yes."

It was over. She wanted to feel relief, the relaxing of her tightly guarded defenses. She could not. She was aware of the slow seep of tiredness through her muscles, along with a niggling feeling that it was too easy, there was something more involved, something she had overlooked.

"Before you go, I would like to tell you once more how much I regret what happened here."

"It doesn't matter." The conventional words rose to her tongue of their own accord. Once spoken, she found they were true.

"It does matter," he said, swinging toward her. "It matters because what happened affects the way you feel. It matters because everything started out wrong, because I want desperately to set things right and there is no other way I can convince you to let me try. Dear God—"

There was the raw note of a prayer in his last words, and then he reached to pull her to him. His lips burned on hers with the fever of his longing. They tasted of wine and remorse and the sweetness of leashed desire. His arms around her were steely in their strength. Kelly felt the leap of the blood in her veins, felt her senses reel. She knew herself to be slipping into a sensuous lassitude where time and place and purpose ceased to exist, and did nothing to stop it. There was no resistance in her hands as she lifted them to his shoulders. As his kiss deepened, her soft lips parted. She felt his hands smoothing over her back, drawing her closer. His fingers touched the nape of her neck, tangling in the soft mass of her hair before they trailed along the angle of her jaw and downward over her shoulder to the curve of her breast. His mouth brushed fire over the gentle plane of her cheek to the sensitive lobes of her ears. He explored the tender and vulnerable curve of her neck, descending with searing suddenness to the pulse that throbbed in the hollow of her throat. His fingers slid beneath the narrow strap of her tank top, slipping it from her shoulder.

"Charles," she breathed, a soft sound not of protest, but of wonder. She pressed closer to him, and was still not close enough.

"Kelly, *chérie,* I love you. *Je t'aime,*" he whispered, his breath warm against the honeyed sweetness of her lips. "Tell me you feel the same."

Love. The word sent a shaft of cold horror through her, banishing her languor. She couldn't love a man like Charles Duralde. She couldn't. And even if she did, he must not know.

"Charles, no!"

"It may be too much to ask, so soon, but if you will see me later, when we leave here, I will make you care."

There was such agony in his voice it brought an ache to her chest. "I can't," she said wildly. "I—I hate you."

"You don't mean that. Sometimes when you look at me, when I hold you, I think you care more than you know."

He was a criminal, without ethics or morals, one who had no concept of the rights of others, but who could imprison them, speak of their deaths without the least sign of compunction. He had said once that he had plans for her. Were they any different now that he claimed to love her, would they change since she had resisted him?

"No, you're wrong!" she cried, breathless with the pain the words gave her.

His hands moved to her arms and he gave her a small shake. "Then why do you smile at me so, why do you come close to me?"

"Because I had to," she cried. "I was pretending, hoping you wouldn't watch me so closely, or at least that you would let me live, set me free when you leave here!"

He flinched as if he had been struck. "I suspected, once, but I couldn't, wouldn't believe it!"

"You had better believe it because it's the truth!"

"You win, Kelly," he said, his tone strained. "To-morrow you'll be free, but there's still tonight."

He crushed her to him, his mouth coming down on hers with bruising force. Her lips burned. Dread and anguish beat up into her mind. She spread her hands against his chest, pushing with all her strength, but could not break his merciless grasp. A shudder ran over her, and hard upon it another and then another until she was trembling uncontrollably. A low sob

146

caught in her throat, and on her lips was the taste of salt tears.

Abruptly he released her, lifting his head, removing his hands as if the touch of her seared him. In the quiet, their ragged breathing was the only sound.

Kelly surged to her feet, flinging away from him toward the screen door. It flew open under her hand to crash against the wire of the veranda, setting it to humming.

"No! Kelly, don't go out there!"

She paid no heed to his shout, but stumbled down the steps and ran headlong into the waiting darkness. She turned toward the lake with its encircling trees, her eyes blinded by the night and her tears. Behind her, she heard Charles's soft curse, and his swift steps as he came after her.

She reached up to clear her vision, wiping her eyes with the palm of her hand. Ahead of her she saw a movement, and she slowed with a gasp of pent-up breath that made her lungs ache. Then she saw him, the shape of a man silhouetted by the moon-silvered brightness of the lake. He was in a crouch, with a rifle slung from the fingers of one hand. As he realized she had stopped, he came an erect, tall, thin figure nestling the scoped rifle against his cheek, pointing it not at her but at the man on the walk behind her.

"No!" she screamed, spinning around. "Charles, go back! Go back!"

She careened into him and they went down as the lake echoed to a cracking explosion of sound. Clamped tightly together, they rolled down the slope and into the deep shade of the live oaks. Suddenly the world was filled with the bright glare of lights and the strident whine of sirens. Bull horns roared, followed by the bursting crackle of shots and the sound of gunned motors as cars raced from around the house.

"This is the police! We have you surrounded. Lay

down your weapons and come out with your hands up!"

Kelly heard the words in despair. With her eyes tightly shut, she lay in Charles's arms, feeling the firm and steady beat of his heart where her cheek rested against his chest. Her clothing was damp with dew from the wet grass. There was a small branch from one of the oaks overhead gouging into her side. Still, the warm shadows enclosed them, an ally hiding them in their comforting darkness. For this brief space of time they were safe. And then she heard the sound of running footsteps, coming toward them.

"Mr. Duralde? Are you all right?"

A flashlight played over them. Charles raised himself to one elbow. The voice, tight with anxiety, belonged to George.

"Yes, I'm fine. I think we both are."

"Lord, but you gave us a scare. That dude nearly plugged you. I don't know what the idea was, you two running out like that, but I'll have to hand this to you. When you create a diversion, you do a bang-up job!"

Without looking at the man who held her, Kelly pulled away from him, coming to her knees. The scene before her had changed with unbelievable swiftness. State troopers, men of the Louisiana State Police, were everywhere. Police cars with their lights flashing, headlights bright, and two-way radios issuing staccato announcements were parked at odd angles all around the house. One man, the tall, thin gunman she had seen, lay writhing on the ground while a trooper worked over him. Two others were being relieved of their rifles and taken into custody. On the veranda the senator had appeared, looking a little dazed as if awakened from sleep. No one was paying the least attention to him, or to Charles.

Still, it was a moment before it struck her. There was a good reason why they were not interested in Charles Duralde. She did not know what he was, nor why he was at the lake house with the senator, but of one thing she was certain. He was not, nor had he ever been, a criminal.

In an amazingly short time, the men had been rounded up and put into the patrol cars, the state police had climbed inside, and all except one of the vehicles were backed down the road and sent speeding out of sight.

"Duralde, are you coming?" the highest-ranking officer called out to Charles as he prepared to step into the final car.

Charles turned from where he stood with Kelly, George, and the senator in a group. "Can't it wait until morning?"

"You know how it is. The sheriff's office here in this parish will be swarming with high-powered lawyers in the next hour. Unless we move fast, they'll have these guys out on bail before sunup."

"I'll be right with you."

Charles turned to Kelly, scanning her pale face there in the headlights of the police car before he let his dark gaze run over her slim figure in stained jeans. "Are you sure you're not hurt?"

"I'm fine," she said, not for the first time.

"There's nothing to be afraid of here, not now."

"I know that," she answered, her voice low.

"George will be staying with you, and the senator."

"We sure will," George chimed in, giving a vigorous nod.

Kelly gave the man she had thought of all this time as the guard a slight smile, then with an effort lifted her gray eyes to meet Charles's dark gaze. "I'll be all right. You don't have to worry."

He reached out, and with a gentle touch removed a leaf that was caught in her hair. "I won't be long."

"There's no hurry," she said, lifting her chin.

A muscle corded in his cheek and his eyes narrowed,

149

then abruptly he turned away. He stepped into the waiting car, slamming the door. It reversed, swinging around Kelly's small car before it shot down the drive and disappeared with a final wink of red taillights.

"Well, now that the excitement is over, shall we go inside?" the senator said.

George nodded, a faint movement in the moonlit dimness. "I could use a drink. This riding to the rescue is enough to give a man a thirst."

"It seems you brought back the cavalry, all right," the other man said. "Though I don't take it kindly that you and Charles didn't see fit to tell me you expected the situation to heat up like this."

"Mr. Duralde was afraid you might try to act the hero, come out where you could be picked off like a sitting duck, instead of staying inside where it was nice and safe."

"I don't much like the idea of other people serving as decoys for me."

"See there? He was pretty certain you wouldn't go for it. But he was sure, from the way these guys acted, that they weren't positive you were here with us. He thought the best thing would be to encourage them to come in for a closer look."

"They might have just shot everyone in sight," the senator objected.

"Yeah. It wasn't in the cards for him and Kelly here to go chasing outside. What happened there, honey?"

It was a moment before Kelly, digesting what they were saying, realized George was speaking to her. "A—misunderstanding."

"Must have been a humdinger for him to let you get away from him like that, but then you've been giving him the devil all week, haven't you?"

The senator, perhaps sensing Kelly's embarrassment, said, "About that drink, there's a beer down at the cottage."

"Sounds fine to me," George said. "How about you, honey?"

"I don't think so," Kelly answered. "You two go ahead."

"Wouldn't you like to come with us, for the company?" the senator suggested.

"I would just as soon be alone, if you don't mind."

"It's not for us to say one way or another, if that's what you want," he returned gently.

"No," George agreed, "but you can be sure Mr. Duralde will have something to say if we leave you by yourself."

"Why? I'm not going anywhere."

"That's not the point. He's the protective sort, and he'll expect me to look after you while he's not here."

"What I do is none of his business."

"Try telling him that."

"I intend to!"

"You probably will. Lord, but I'm not sure which one of you I feel sorriest for."

"You needn't waste your pity on me." Kelly did not wait for an answer, but turned on her heel and made for the steps of the veranda. She did not think George would try to stop her, and she was right. The two men hesitated, talking in low voices. By the time she had reached the living room and began to close the drapes, they were moving off in the direction of the cottage.

Kelly let her shoulders sag as she turned away from the windows. Her wine glass, still half full, sat where she had left it on the end table. She picked it up, lifting it to her lips to taste the pale yellow liquid. It had grown warm, but she drank it anyway, wandering about the room with the glass in her hand.

It was clear that Charles expected her to be there when he got back from filling out a formal complaint against the would-be killers. Whether by accident or design, he had made certain of it by taking her car keys with him. Why couldn't he have left her a way out? She wanted nothing so much as to be gone, to never have to face Charles Duralde again after what had passed between them. She wanted to throw her things into her suitcase and run, putting as much distance as possible between herself and the lake house. She wanted to leave all this behind her, to forget it as quickly and thoroughly as she could.

She felt like such a fool. How had she come to make such a mistake? It had been Charles's attitude, his odd determination to have no one know the whereabouts of the older man, all combined with the phrasing of the words she had overheard between him and George. She was still not certain what was going on, though she was beginning to have an idea. And yet, she would gladly let it remain a mystery forever if it would keep her from having to see Charles again.

Hot embarrassment flooded over her every time she thought of the scene between them on the veranda. A diversion, George had called it. Well, that was as good a word as any. She realized now, looking back, the reason for the open drapes, the loud music, his invitation to dance. He had suspected the men who had been in the boat with the spotlight the night before would be back. He had wanted them to see a couple having a good time, enjoying each other's company. He hadn't wanted her to go outside on the veranda; she remembered that now. But once they were there, he had managed to keep the show interesting. Only she wasn't supposed to take it seriously, she wasn't supposed to have jumped up and run crying into the night.

Had he meant anything he had said, or had he just gotten carried away with his role? He had not liked being told that she had been play-acting. The violence of his kiss still had the power, even in memory, to make her shiver. It was some consolation that she had not allowed him to guess how strongly she was attracted to him. A little, but not much.

What a mess everything was. If Charles had only

trusted her enough to tell her the truth. If she had relied on her instincts that told her he could not be a killer. If she had not let down her guard against him in her attempts to encourage him to grow attached to her. If he had not spoken of love, instead of the physical desire that was all she had expected him to feel. If.

What was the use? She had fallen in love with him. She had allowed him to get past her defenses. Regardless of what he might have felt, she had made him despise her with pretense and distrust. That he had given her ample reason for both made no difference. She would not get a second chance, not in these circumstances. Not that she wanted one, of course.

Tomorrow she could leave. He had promised that much before the excitement started. With any luck, she would do no more than say a quiet and dignified good-bye and depart. He might feel that a few words of explanation were called for, and if so, she would listen, but that was all. She would go without maudlin scenes, without telling him she loved him, and with her pride and self-respect intact.

Moving slowly, leaving the lights in the living room on behind her, Kelly went to her bedroom. She closed the door and set her empty wine glass down on the dresser. She picked up her hairbrush and with sudden fierceness whipped off the blue ribbon and brushed the trash and leaves from the gold-brown waves. That done, she undressed and put on her green nightgown. She washed her face and brushed her teeth. Taking a deep breath, she turned back the covers of the bed and climbed in. It was not what she wanted, but it seemed there was nothing else for her to do. And if warm tears slid from the corners of her eyes to make wet tracks into her hair, who was there to know?

❊ Chapter 10 ❊

Once before this past week she had awakened to the smell of coffee. This seemed a repeat of that time, for the fresh aroma was strong, and there was the glow of morning beyond her closed eyelids. Charles must be up. She burrowed her head into the pillow, unwilling to think of him, unwilling to leave the last gray vestiges of soothing slumber. She had not enjoyed that oblivion for long. She had been awake, staring with burning eyes at the ceiling, when he had returned. He had not gone to bed at once, but had paced about in the front part of the house. It was only after he had finally settled down in the room next to hers that she had been able to doze off. Why he was up again so soon she could not imagine, unless he was determined to see her gone from this place early, before he left himself.

He was an unpredictable man. On the other occasion when she had been brought from sleep by the smell of coffee, he had invaded her room to put the cup on her bedside table, practically under her nose.

Caution asserted itself. At the faint chink of china, her eyes flew open. Charles stood beside her bed, just placing a cup and saucer on the bedside table.

She rolled over, sitting up with a rush, pulling the sheet up over her breasts. "What are you doing?"

He lifted a brow. "That must be obvious."

"Yes," she said, her tone acerbic as she pushed her hair back with her fingers, "but why?"

"I wanted some answers and, as I recall, you respond better to a compromising position than to simple questions."

Indignation flared in her eyes. "That's a terrible thing to say!"

"Isn't it?" he agreed, his smile genial.

"If you are talking about that display of sheer brute strength you put on when you wanted to know my name—"

"You do remember?"

She did, vividly. She was not certain she would ever forget the way he had held her on the couch with his lips fractions of an inch from hers as he had demanded to know her name. The mere thought of it was enough to make her face feel warm. "Why not?" she inquired. "I have never been treated so callously in my life!"

"Maybe, but I don't think it was the brute strength, as you call it, or the callousness, that made you answer."

"Just what was it then?"

"The certainty of what was going to happen if you didn't, something you might keep in mind now."

She sent him a smoldering glance. "It's all very well for you to talk, but if anybody deserves answers, I think I do!"

"Fair enough. Where would you like to start?"

She eyed him suspiciously as he seated himself on the side of her bed. He looked fresh and alert in an open-necked sports shirt and a pair of twill pants, in marked contrast to the way she felt.

He waited a moment, then leaned to pick up her coffee cup, handing it carefully to her across the width of the sheet. As she took it, his dark gaze moved over the tousled glory of her hair, coming to rest on the shadows under her eyes and the look of recent tears. She lowered her lashes, sipping at the hot, aromatic brew colored slightly with cream, just the way she liked it. When she looked up again, she was in time to see the smile that softened the bronzed planes of his face for an instant before it vanished.

At the thought that he might be laughing at her, her lips tightened. "To begin with," she said, her tone hard, "who is the senator, and why are you keeping him here?"

"His name is Landry," Charles answered without hesitation, "and he was a friend of my father's. As to keeping him here, I'm not."

"But you are. George said——"

"Yes? Just what did George say?"

She swallowed, taking another sip of her coffee. "I don't remember exactly."

"I think you remember enough."

She gave him a straight look. "All right. He said that the senator was getting restless and hard to handle, wanting to go home to his family. He said it looked like he should have sense enough to be afraid, and he meant afraid of dying."

"George said this to you?" he asked, frowning.

"I—overheard it."

His face cleared. "I begin to see. And you took what you heard to be proof that we were holding the senator against his will?"

"For a payoff that would come in less than two weeks."

He shook his head. "I know you mentioned the possibility at first, but I thought surely you had rid yourself of the notion by now. Once I even as much as told you it was untrue."

"You can't deny you encouraged me to believe it that first evening. Later you set me a riddle; I could think the best or the worst of you. But that isn't the same as a plain statement of fact."

"And the way he was housed without restraints, cosseted with television, ice cream, meals on trays; didn't that suggest anything?" His black eyes held hers, their expression demanding.

She gave a small shake of her head. "Not compared to what I had heard."

"My God, Kelly, do I look like a kidnapper?"

"Whether you looked like one or not, you certainly acted the part where I was concerned," she said, her tones becoming heated. "You wouldn't let me talk to him. You forced me to stay here after you knew I had seen him. You wouldn't tell me who you were, or what you were up to; what did you expect?"

"I expected you to believe what I told you, that you were safe, that what I was doing was for your own good, and that you would be free as soon as possible!"

"And I was supposed to take your word, just like that, without explanation or knowing the first thing about you? Doesn't that strike you as being a little high-handed?"

"At least you left me in no doubt that it struck you that way," he said grimly, then held up his hand as she started to answer. "No, wait, let me think this through. It changes the whole problem."

The minutes ticked past. Kelly tried to conceal the faint trembling of her hands by holding on to her coffee cup. She glanced at Charles, at the frown that drew his brows together. Her heart seemed to contract in her chest, and she looked away once more.

He drained his coffee cup and set it on the table before he turned to her. "All right. Let's take this from the beginning. You know who my father was?"

"A friend of Judge Kavanaugh?"

"Yes, and also of the senator, though that's not what I am getting at. He was a politician, of sorts. At one time he ran for office and was elected as representative of his district. Once in the state capital at Baton Rouge, however, he found his sphere of influence limited. Too, he ran into the public's attitude toward elected officials as all of them being in it for what they can get."

"I see," Kelly murmured. That explained the reference George had made that morning to the time when old man Duralde, Charles's father, had been in Baton Rouge, and of the railroad spur and post office that had a part of the operation, whatever that was, at the time.

"When his term ended, he refused to run for reelection, but still maintained a certain influence behind the scenes. He was—not a poor man, and he had a strong sense of fair play. He made it his business for quite a few years to see to it that the political machine in his section of the state kept its nose clean. After thirty or forty years, he knew most of the people in public office, knew their strengths and weaknesses and backgrounds, knew who was suited for what post, and who wasn't."

"A king-maker."

"Not exactly, since he had nothing personal to gain, but I suppose that description comes as close as anything."

"That's interesting, of course, but I don't see what it has to do with the senator and why he is here."

"I'm coming to that. Senator Landry is in a position a great deal like that of my father, except that he never ran in a public campaign. He was once appointed to fill the unexpired term of a senator who died in office, however. He declined to try for a full term, but he enjoys the honorary title and he likes to stay involved in the political game."

"A pair of king-makers."

"If you like, though their interference in the democratic process was limited to supporting the man they felt to be best qualified for the job and lining up other support, helping arrange financing, planning strategy. There was nothing underhanded or illegal about it, just a nice, clean fight decided by the voters. Until the last two election campaigns."

Was this the reason he had been interested in her opinion on the subjects of money and politics? She could not see what difference it made what she thought. Perhaps it had been an idle question, an attempt to find some common ground between them for conversation, and nothing more? It did not follow that because he had asked what she thought, he had a personal interest in her answer. Realizing, suddenly, that her mind was wandering, she tried to pick up the thread of what he had been saying.

"I read something about the elections scandals in that area during the last campaign."

He nodded, the look in his eyes somber. "My father suspected from the first that organized crime was behind it. He and the senator set out to prove it, and to expose the fraud. They succeeded. The whole thing was blown wide open; corruption, vote buying, illegal contributions, the underworld connection, the whole dirty deal. The media got wind of it and put a bright light on the operation. People were arrested and brought before the grand jury where they were indicted and bound over for trial. My father and the senator were called as witnesses."

Kelly stared at him with horror in her eyes as she recognized the trend of his story. "And then your father was killed in an accident."

"Only it wasn't an accident. His car was deliberately forced off the road and into a canal. An attempt was made on the life of the senator, but he was luckier. After that, he was given police protection. The officer guarding him nearly let a sniper make good at his second attempt. There was some doubt as to how hard he had tried to provide protection, and the question arose of a possible bribe being passed. It became clear that

159

something had to be done. I had a special interest in seeing that the men behind the death of my father were brought to justice. More than that, Landry was my father's friend; I had known him all my life. I thought of the judge, and this place, and so we came here."

It made beautiful sense, once you knew, though there were still a number of things she didn't understand. "How does the payoff come into it?" she asked, her brows drawn together as she stared at him. "I'm sure I didn't make that up."

"If memory serves me right, I was talking about a payoff not in money, but in justice that would come as soon as the case went to trial. That would be after this week, on Monday when court reconvenes for the fall, or at least when the evidence that the senator has to present is given, in two weeks at the most."

Her gray eyes were still troubled as she tilted her head to one side. "I don't mean to sound like a lawyer, but isn't it a little unusual for a judge to try a case where he has given shelter to a witness for the prosecution?"

"You mean Judge Kavanaugh? The case will be tried out of his district. His only connection with it has been his interest in seeing my father's killers brought to justice, and the loan of his house for a place of safekeeping. He was more than a little concerned when he heard that you were mixed up in the business. It was all I could do to keep him from flying home to talk to you. He sent instructions that I should tell you the truth and rely on your good sense, but George had neglected to explain to him just how angry I had made you. I wasn't too sure that seeing me in trouble wouldn't have suited you just fine."

"You don't really think that?" There was a distressed look on her face as she stared at him.

"Maybe not, though I wouldn't have given two cents for my chances after that episode when we went fishing."

She looked down at her empty cup, rolling it back and forth in her hands. "I can see how my arriving on the scene might have been an inconvenience."

"Inconvenience? That's a gross understatement. We had been here a week with absolutely no problems, everything placid and peaceful as anybody could wish, and then you came. When I found you climbing in that window, I saw red. It seemed just barely possible that whoever was after the senator had connected his disappearance with me. If they had tracked me down, it was likely they would send somebody to check out the place. Women are taking their place in the ranks of crime these days, as in everything else. Why not an attractive girl as a plant, a member of the mob? It almost seemed more plausible than that story you gave me. I couldn't believe Judge Kavanaugh wouldn't have seen to it that we would be left undisturbed. I hadn't counted on his gentlemanly protection of his wife and daughter by keeping them in the dark."

"I don't see why not. Wasn't that part of the reason why you didn't see fit to tell me what was going on? So the men who were after the senator, if they overran the place, could be told I didn't know a thing about it, as if that were going to make any difference."

"I suppose you could look at it like that," he said stiffly.

"On the other hand, you kept me here because you thought that if you let me go I would run all over the country talking to one and all about the man I saw hiding here. Just as the judge probably thought Mary and his wife wouldn't be able to keep the secret, if the truth were known. You men are all alike, keeping women in ignorance to protect them, when all you are doing is leaving yourselves, and us, open to danger because of what we don't know!"

"Wait a minute. Are you saying that if I had told you everything you would have stayed on here and, shall we say, added to the local color?"

"I might have," she admitted. "At least I would have done a better job of pretending to be your—your special friend than you managed to convey without my cooperation!"

"I don't know about that; I thought we did well enough."

She ignored that, as well as the smile that went with his amused comment. "While I'm on the subject, you can tell me just what the idea was of saying last night that I could leave today, when all the time you knew those gunmen were sneaking up on the house."

"I didn't know; I only suspected after the odd behavior of the boat we saw the evening before. I'm not sure how they located us, unless it was as I said, that they made the connection between me and the senator, then maybe had a tip about George from one of his trips with the speedboat. Yesterday afternoon, when the three of us were in conference, we decided it was time to move; the only question was where. The senator wanted to go home. George was for a hotel in New Orleans. I took a lot of ribbing for proposing we commandeer your apartment. We couldn't agree, so we put it off until morning."

"And in the meantime, you set yourself, and me, up as decoys, creating a diversion while the police moved in."

"It was doubtful which was more dangerous, staying put, or trying to move when we suspected strongly that our cover had been blown. Calling in reinforcements seemed wisest. As for setting you up, would you have gone to your room and stayed there if I had asked you?"

"If there was a good reason."

"You'll have to admit, at least, that you had done nothing up till then to make me think you might. That being the case, I preferred to keep you with me."

"So you could watch me."

"So I could watch over you; there's a difference. I

162

sent George for the police early enough so they could get in place before trouble started. I thought you would be safe enough as long as you remained inside. I certainly didn't expect you to leave the house."

She would just as soon not go into her reason for doing that. "I suppose you are going to say that what I ran into was my own fault, then?"

"I wouldn't be so ungallant."

"Wouldn't you?" she inquired in bitter disbelief. "And I guess you blame me for all those trips George made in the speedboat, trying to find out who I was."

"No. It wasn't a good idea to let him use the speedboat. Neither it, nor George for that matter, blend in with a place like this."

That was a concession. She made a small grimace. "I thought he was a guard."

"He was a federal agent at one time, before he became my father's chauffeur. He asked to come with me to help look after the senator here because he blames himself, at least in part, for my father's death. It was George's night off, the evening he was killed. Dad hadn't planned to go out, but he had a call, bogus of course, and he went, alone."

"Was he at the farm, or whatever it is, above New Orleans?"

There was a shading of self-blame in Charles's voice also, she thought.

"The plantation? Yes, he was spending a few days there. I had gone into the city for the evening. Calls in the night aren't too unusual with the kind of agricultural-industrial complex we keep going, but if I had been there, I would have taken the call."

"Whoever killed him must have known you weren't there."

He reached up to rake his fingers through his hair, letting out his breath in a long sigh. "I guess so."

"I'm sorry," she said, looking down at the coffee cup

she still turned in her hands. "I really am, for everything."

"If you mean about my father's death, I'll accept that. As for the rest, don't be. I'm not."

In a denial of the compassion that sought to weaken her defenses, she allowed a glint of anger to creep into her gray eyes. "Well, you should be! When I think of the things you did, it makes me want to—scream."

"It's a little late for that, isn't it?"

Something in his voice made her aware, abruptly, of the fact that they were alone in the house, and that this was a man she had not known existed only a week before. Moreover, there he sat on her bed, watching her as if he had a perfect right to be in her bedroom. It was also a matter for concern that although she was disturbed by the sheer masculinity of his presence, she wasn't particularly embarrassed by it. Considering how she would have reacted not too long ago, that was shocking if not too surprising after what had passed between them.

"I suppose so," she murmured at last.

"Besides, you aren't the one with the scars."

She flicked a glance at the place where his lip had been cut, now nearly healed, then looked away again. "I wish I had left more."

"Maybe you did, with your play-acting, pretending to be coming around, to be falling for me."

"I wasn't the only one! What about the things you said and did on the veranda in full view of who knows how many people?"

He smiled, his dark eyes bright. "Does that rankle, that I didn't mean it? Or is it the public performance that you object to?"

"I was only pointing out that you aren't exactly an innocent party," she said, sitting up higher in the bed. "As to objecting, I don't suppose I can, that much, since it was in a good cause."

"An extremely reasonable attitude. I'm glad you absolve me of blame. On the other hand, I'm not quite so forgiving."

"What—what do you mean?" she asked, suspicion threading her tone.

"I'm talking about our truce. You were supposed to relax and stop fighting me. You trusted me, remember?"

The soft timbre of his voice sent a shiver along her spine. "You can't condemn me for using the only means I had left to get around you when I had no idea what you meant to do."

"Do? I told you that you were safe."

"But you certainly didn't act like it, and I heard you tell George that you had plans for me. That didn't sound like anything I wanted to stick around for."

He frowned, then his teeth flashed in a grim smile. "I meant to take you fishing, and generally put you on view to make our being here less conspicuous, as three males keeping to themselves."

"How could I know that?" She slanted him a look dark with resentment.

"You couldn't, but you still didn't have to break our truce, especially after you had been warned."

Kelly tried for a light laugh. "All that is over now. It doesn't matter anymore."

"Oh, but it does." He reached out to take the cup from her hand and set it aside. His movements were slow and almost menacing.

She moistened her lips with the tip of her tongue. "Why? What difference does it make?"

"You gave me your promise, and you broke it. If I let you get away with this, how can I trust you in more important matters?"

"To me, it was a question of life or death. I don't like to be melodramatic, but how much more important can it get?"

"It was life or death for me, too; my father's, the

165

senator's." He caught her wrist in his strong fingers, drawing her toward him.

"Charles," she said with a catch in her voice, "don't."

"You smiled at me, all sweetness and provocation, with such a warm glow in your eyes. You brushed against me with such touching innocence, as if you had no idea what you were doing to me. I wanted you. I dared to hope, and you let me because that was what you wanted all the time. For me to hope. That was your greatest mistake."

"No."

His arms closed around her, their grip like iron bands. His eyes burned into her with the darkness of desire. She could feel the hard beat of his heart, and the suffocating throb of her own as he pulled her across his lap and, with slow strength, lowered her to the bed on her back. As he hovered above her braced on one elbow, she knew a treacherous weakness, a longing to close her eyes and accept what would come.

"Please, Charles," she whispered, and was not sure for what she pleaded.

"There is one thing that may be in your favor," he told her, his voice taut and low. "When I followed you from the veranda, when you saw the man with the gun, you called out something to me. What was it?"

She stared up at him, trying to think. "It was—I don't know."

"I think you do, Kelly. Tell me."

"I—only told you to go back."

"You warned me of danger, even when you thought I was a kidnapper, or worse?"

"I guess so," she answered, lowering her lashes.

"You know so. Why, Kelly? Tell me why?"

Closing her eyes tightly, she shook her head. "I can't."

"You can, and you will, if you know what's good for—both of us."

The strain in his tone communicated itself to Kelly. She opened her eyes, seeing the pain mirrored in his dark gaze, and the uncertainty. It was the latter, so out of character for him, that touched her, bringing the shimmer of tears she could not hide.

"*Chérie*," he breathed, "dear God, don't cry."

"I can't help it," she said, her voice breaking. "It seems to be— the way loving you—affects me."

"Ah, *chérie*." He crushed her to him, rocking her slowly in his arms. "It was no act when I said I loved you. *Je t'adore*, I adore you. Nothing could be more real than that to me. When I said those words I had forgotten everything except what I felt for you and how beautiful you were."

His mouth found hers then in a kiss that was warm, and edged with tender passion, carefully leashed. His hand cupped her face, and between soft murmurs of love in two languages, he brushed his lips over her forehead, her eyelids, the tip of her nose, and downward over her throat.

"Charles?" she said, slowly running her fingers over the back of his neck. "If I had not said I loved you—"

He stopped her there, irresistibly drawn to that word on her lips.

"If I hadn't said it," she persevered when she had breath, "what would you have done?"

He went still. "I don't know. I will show you what I wanted to do, had planned to do, after we are married."

"Are we going to be married?"

"But of course."

She did not mind at all, she found, the arrogance of his tone, though it would be best if he didn't know it. "I don't remember being asked."

He raised his head so he could look at her, a smile lurking in his eyes. "Do you want to be—knowing my method of assuring I get the answer I want to hear?"

"Would it be so terrible if I said yes?" She shielded

her gaze with her lashes, though she did not miss the leap of flame deep in his eyes.

"It would be enchanting."

"Well?"

"I think I will deny you the privilege, for both our sakes."

She worked that out in her mind. "I'm not sure I like that."

"I was hoping you wouldn't."

"If I don't get a proposal, do I still get to marry you?"

"It's mandatory."

"That sounds as if I don't have a choice."

"Call it the consequences of breaking our truce. You will never get away from me."

With the tip of one finger and a feather touch, she traced along his cheek, then around the chiseled outline of his mouth. "Suppose I don't want to—get away, I mean?"

He gave a sigh of mock despair. "Is there no way I can punish you as you deserve?"

"Yes," she whispered, her gray eyes wide, "don't kiss me."

It was, of course, an impossible condition.

SIGNET Books You'll Enjoy

- [ ] **SIGNET DOUBLE ROMANCE—WEB OF ENCHANTMENT** by Claudia Slack and **OUTRAGEOUS FORTUNE** by Claudia Slack. (#J9357—$1.95)
- [ ] **ALOHA TO LOVE** by Mary Ann Taylor. (#E8765—$1.75)*
- [ ] **HAWAIIAN INTERLUDE** by Mary Ann Taylor. (#E9031—$1.75)
- [ ] **SIGNET DOUBLE ROMANCE—ROMANCE IN THE HEADLINES** by Mary Ann Taylor and **BON VOYAGE, MY DARLING** by Mary Ann Taylor. (#J9175—$1.95)
- [ ] **LOVER'S REUNION** by Arlene Hale. (#W7771—$1.50)
- [ ] **A STORMY SEA OF LOVE** by Arlene Hale. (#W7938—$1.50)
- [ ] **A VOTE FOR LOVE** by Arlene Hale. (#Y7505—$1.25)
- [ ] **EVIE'S ROMAN FORTUNE** by Joanna Bristol. (#W8616—$1.50)*
- [ ] **EVIE'S FORTUNE IN PARIS** by Joanna Bristol. (#W8267—$1.50)*
- [ ] **FORTUNES OF EVIE** by Joanna Bristol. (#W7982—$1.50)*
- [ ] **FURY'S SUN, PASSION'S MOON** by Gimone Hall. (#E8748—$2.50)*
- [ ] **RAPTURE'S MISTRESS** by Gimone Hall. (#E8422—$2.25)*
- [ ] **GIFTS OF LOVE** by Charlotte Vale Allen. (#J8388—$1.95)*
- [ ] **MOMENTS OF MEANING** by Charlotte Vale Allen. (#J8817—$1.95)*
- [ ] **TIMES OF TRIUMPH** by Charlotte Vale Allen. (#E8955—$2.50)*

* Price slightly higher in Canada

Buy them at your local
bookstore or use coupon
on next page for ordering.

SIGNET Books by Glenna Finley

☐	**AFFAIRS OF LOVE**	(#E9409—$1.75)*
☐	**THE MARRIAGE MERGER**	(#E8391—$1.75)*
☐	**WILDFIRE OF LOVE**	(#E8602—$1.75)*
☐	**BEWARE MY HEART**	(#E9192—$1.75)
☐	**BRIDAL AFFAIR**	(#E9058—$1.75)
☐	**THE CAPTURED HEART**	(#W8310—$1.50)
☐	**DARE TO LOVE**	(#E8992—$1.75)
☐	**HOLIDAY FOR LOVE**	(#E9093—$1.75)
☐	**KISS A STRANGER**	(#W8308—$1.50)
☐	**LOVE FOR A ROGUE**	(#E8741—$1.75)
☐	**LOVE IN DANGER**	(#E9190—$1.75)
☐	**LOVE'S HIDDEN FIRE**	(#E9191—$1.75)
☐	**LOVE LIES NORTH**	(#E8740—$1.75)
☐	**LOVE'S MAGIC SPELL**	(#W7849—$1.50)
☐	**A PROMISING AFFAIR**	(#W7917—$1.50)
☐	**THE RELUCTANT MAIDEN**	(#Y6781—$1.25)
☐	**THE ROMANTIC SPIRIT**	(#E8780—$1.75)
☐	**STORM OF DESIRE**	(#E8777—$1.75)
☐	**SURRENDER MY LOVE**	(#Y7916—$1.50)
☐	**TREASURE OF THE HEART**	(#Y7324—$1.25)
☐	**WHEN LOVE SPEAKS**	(#Y7597—$1.25)

* Price slightly higher in Canada
